SO-AXL-221

CIRCLE
OF
SEASONS

CIRCLE

OF

SEASONS

by Ann Nolan Clark

ILLUSTRATED BY W. T. MARS

A BELL BOOK
Farrar, Straus & Giroux, New York

To my grandchildren
Pat and Mary Clark
and
my great-grandchildren
Patrick and Stacy Clark

In most of the pueblos the calendar year is in two parts. These divisions are the Days of the Winter, which are kept by the Winter Chief for the Winter People, and the Days of the Summer, kept by the Summer Chief for the Summer People.

Within the Days of the Winter and the Days of the Summer are seasonal times of secret and sacred rites as well as public dance ceremonials, fiestas, and seasonal activities.

I describe only those events which some Pueblo group has shared with me by permitting me to participate in them, to watch them, or to be told about them. Most of these events are of the Tewa people, a branch of the Tanoan language group, but also recorded are a few ceremonials of the Tigua and Keres groups. I write only of the things I remember, as the Pueblo children's teacher and friend and as neighbor of the Pueblo people.

Ann Nolan Clark

Contents

CONTENTS

CIRCLE
OF
SEASONS

Foreword

Today, in the upper Rio Grande Valley of New Mexico, there are fifteen Indian villages on or near the banks of the river. To the west of the river are three more, and on the tops of three high mesas in Arizona there are the Hopi groups. They are known as the Pueblo Indians, a name given them by the early Spanish explorers because they found the Indians living in compact, well-governed, town-like communities. All the villages were built on the same plan; all the houses were made of sun-dried brick or hand-cut stone. The houses were terraced in many stories, their walls connecting and enclosing inner plazas. In these plazas much of the common activities of the village was carried on.

In early Spanish times there were more of these villages than at present; they were larger and more densely populated. But the ones that have outlasted the years of conquest have changed little and are still the same sites that the Spanish visited. Indians had been occupying these sites for five hundred years before the coming of the Spanish, and their ancestors had lived in the nearby region for many centuries before that. These ancestors were growing crops, knew about irrigation and the fertilizing of their fields, and had a system of government and spiritual ceremonials at the time of the Birth of Christ. Although the traditions and organizations of the different villages were similar, they did not have the same origin. They came of four distinct language groups and have kept these languages separate for a thousand years or more. The people of each village still speak their own mother tongue. The languages they have in common with other villages are Spanish and English.

Today the groups differ slightly in appearance, characteristics, dress, crafts, and customs. A custom of one village is not necessarily the same in other villages, but there is the same general plan.

Not all Pueblo Indians live in their home villages. Many live in other parts of the United States and do the same kinds of work and live in the same manner as other American citizens. They return to their home village often, where their land, their houses, their horse herds, and their place in the social and ceremonial life of the village have been kept for them, a sacred trust. When these wayfarers return, they are one with the tribesmen who have not chosen to leave the home hearths. How long this will be true cannot be foretold. The moving force of change in the outside world may tomorrow blur the trails of the Ancients, although they have been cut deep in time.

Pueblo Indians are gentle, kindly, laughter-loving people. Seeing them mold their clay pots, turn the

4

brown earth of their fields, coax the slow dribble of water through the little feeder ditches to irrigate their corn, the stranger thinks of them as people living placid, humdrum lives that are seasoned only by moments of laughter. Not knowing them, this is what the stranger thinks. But under the surface of this outward calm and patient acceptance is a deep, lasting, sensitive, spiritual way of life.

A Pueblo Indian lives by his days, and as each day is lived, so shapes his year. A day is not an unplanned happening, not merely a new dawn following the sunset of yesterday. It is not entirely the possession of the person who lives it, but a trust that he holds in common with his tribesmen for their common good. A day is not to be met with an untried approach toward an untested goal. Each individual must hold to a common guideline, taut and strong, that reaches into the present from the distant past. Each day has been determined and patterned by the cumulative wisdom of the Ancients, who walked, uncounted centuries ago, along this same trail of Pueblo living. It has been determined by ritual and patterned by tradition, formed not by man-made laws—arbitrary and artificial—but by natural laws that are in harmony with the Earth Mother who gave them being.

Each pueblo is divided into two groups of people known as the Summer and the Winter, or the Turquoise and the Squash, People. Children belong to the people of their mother. Each group has its head, the Summer Chief or the Winter Chief, and each group supervises the seasonal activities and ceremonies under the spiritual and traditional direction of its chief. The Indians say that the Winter (or the Summer) Chief keeps the days for the people. By this they mean that the chief records the passing of the days, foretells the coming of certain ceremonies, and blesses the days under his supervision by fasting, prayer, and ceremonial rituals that have been handed down by tradition. Time is reckoned by the light of the moon and the stars of the night and by the shadows the sun leaves on mesa top, mountain peak, or canyon walls. The chiefs record the days in their passing by painted lines or rows of stones or little mounds of bones, and they make no error, for each day has its special place and its prescribed ritual and its seasonal message. The seasons are the lawgivers, and obedience to these laws means a continuing life for the people. The day is the heartbeat in the time span of the season. The season is the flow of blood in the life stream of the people. So all the days are important. No one day is set aside in reverence to the Life Power. Every day is a day of reverence. Every thought, every need, every act is dedicated to the Holder-of-the-Trails-of-Life and asks the help of the sun and the land and the rain for the good of all of the people. Nothing is begun without asking this blessing —wakening in the morning, lighting the cook fire,

6

firing the clay pots, preparing the earth for seed planting—everything has its special ritual. All these rituals are sacred, many of them secret, magical, and mysterious.

So the seasons circle, bringing each year to rich fulfillment. Prayer, ceremonial, retreat, laughter, fiesta, work make the year-song of the lifeway of a simple, pastoral, strong, and good people, a song with its melody ringing clear and true, neither distorted nor muted by the mists of the past.

THE
DAYS
OF
THE
WINTER

*****

Time of Seasonal Transfer

Days are gold-filled with sunshine and sun warmth; nights are lightly blanketed in blue velvet studded with the light of a million stars. Crops have been harvested. Seed plants have been put away in the keeping-places blessed to receive them. Winter food has been dried and hung in the storerooms of the pueblo houses. The year that was is ending.

Now comes a time of overlapping when the Sun Chief and the Winter Chief hold jointly the year-circle that encloses their people. This is the time when the days of the year are about to be transferred from the trust of one chief to the trust of the other. In the pueblos this is not a quiet interlude between the labors of autumn and the hardships of winter. This is not a time of resting but a time of intense observation by the Keepers of the Pueblo Year and a time of reverent waiting by those whose days are kept for them by their Year Fathers.

During this time the Summer Chief stays in the House of the Summer People. The Winter Chief stays in the House of the Winter People. Each one, according to the pattern handed down to him by his Ancients, watches and records the day shadows of sunrise and sunset upon a certain place or thing. He watches and records the positions of the stars in the sky at night. By his side are his prayer fetishes, his sacred corn meal, his bowl of medicine water, and his tallies for recording.

In some pueblos this time of retreat lasts for twelve days. At other villages it is of shorter duration, but in all of them it is a time of meditation and preparation for change. The relationship between the Pueblo Indians and their environment is close and complete, and as the landscape around them changes from the lushness of autumn to the bleakness of winter, so do the people change. It is at this time that they make their inner beings ready for the new year that comes upon them. This is a solemn time, but it is not an anxious time, for the people know that at a certain hour, both light and shadow, and the sun, moon, and stars will have made known to the chiefs that summer has been completed and winter has begun. They know then that the days to come will not be in the Summer Chief's holding but will be kept for them by the Winter Chief. They know this; their Ancients have told them. And so it comes to pass: that pause in time when summer gives way to winter.

The ceremony of transfer is not shared with non-Indians. It is only for the Indians. It is only for people who know that Sun is the all-father and Earth is the all-mother. Only they can understand, value, and sanctify it.

Winter solstice, "when the Sun in his house rests," does not immediately follow the transfer. There is a period of waiting until this event takes place. Whether this time of waiting is needed for the appearance of the right sign and omens foretelling solstice, or for the slow unfolding of the ceremonies and rituals leading to the climax of solstice, is not talked about. There is no need to talk about it. The Indians know that the transfer has been made and that solstice in its own good time will follow.

* * * * *

Day of the Dead

Snow clouds shroud the peaks of the Sangre de Cristo Mountains. Sun hides his face. Silence hangs heavy over the land, the dry arroyos, the barren fields. Only a trickle of water moves over the stones in the river bed. Only a little wind moves among the dead leaves of the cottonwood trees by the banks of the river.

It seems but yesterday that sun blessed the purple mountains, the red earth, the pink sandhills, the green stunted piñon, the smoke-gray cedar. It seems but yesterday that the village was a rainbow of colors as harvest crops dried in the autumn sun! It was a rainbow of sounds, the laughter of a happy people bringing their year to its fruitful completion.

Between yesterday and today the mood of the sun and the land and the people has changed. Today the pueblo is closed. A thin rope of rawhide lies on the sand of the road by the river bridge, sign to friend and stranger alike that today this road is closed. Tewa people stay inside their houses; doors are shut. The white man's world on the other side of the river does not exist. It is as if it never was.

Today the Tewas' thoughts turn inward, turn backward to the way of their Ancients. Today the Tewas' thoughts turn to those of their blood who have gone on the long trail to the Spirit World. For a day and a night the people of life welcome back the people of death to the world of the living. This is not a day of sorrow or of tears or of mourning. It is a day of rejoicing. Departed loved ones must be made to know that they have not been forgotten. They have been remembered; their places have been kept for them in the hearts and ways of their people.

Although the entire pueblo observes this special time, in many ways it is a family ceremony rather than a group one. Each family welcomes back to the family hearth loved ones from the spirit world. In each home a feast is prepared for them, all the favorite food cooked in the ways they liked best. The respected Old Father of each family receives this food-offering from the older family members and in prescribed and solemn ritual releases the spirit of the food to satisfy the spirit-hunger of those spirit-beings who once were flesh and bone.

In some pueblos, crops are brought to the door of the Christian church to be looked upon with favor by the Christian God whose house it is, and some of the fruits of the harvest are left there for the good Padre who ministers to the Christian needs of the people.

This welcoming-back time is a day of prayer-offering, Christian and pagan, from the world of reality to the world of the spirits. It is a day of beautiful and mystic communion between those who are and those who were. Each hour passes, true to the pattern which has been determined and fixed by the Ancients.

When a new dawn again lightens the pueblo world, it finds a people happy and at peace, comforted by the visit of their departed loved ones, and serene in the acceptance that death is a transition, not an ending.

＊ ＊ ＊ ＊ ＊

Fiesta

Sunrise sky is streaked with gold and scarlet; the air is frost-filled, sparkling, and lightly touched with cold. Only the tips of the Sangre de Cristo peaks, edged with new snow, can be seen above the blue mist that hangs heavy in the foothills of the mountain range, hiding the sand dunes, softening the stubble in the fields, filling the dry arroyos. Night shadows still lurk in the narrow passageways under the portals and against the house walls. Night silence still holds the mud-brown village in a pocket of quiet in the misted blue morning.

But the people in the pueblo are not asleep. Even before Sun Father has shone his face in the gap between the mountain peaks, even before the house doors are open, the work of the day has begun for the people. Smoke curls upward from squat chimneys to merge with the mist and the shadows. Smells of fried bread swelling to puff balls in bubbling fat, coffee boiling in enamel coffee pots, and burning piñon wood blend in an incense offering to the new day.

A blanketed figure appears on the flat roof of one of the houses, the town crier, greeting the day and the people and announcing the work of the day. The pueblo comes alive, buzzing with the noises of morning. Some-

where a dog barks, a baby cries, a horse neighs. There is the sound of laughter and a young man sings a snatch of song.

House doors open. Blanketed men, and boys in school sweaters, walk across the plaza, through the passageways, to the night corral. They saddle their horses, hitch teams to their wagons, and go in a long line across the bridge, along the sandy road, by the fenced fields, around the sand dunes, through the deep arroyos, to the foothills of the mountains. They are going for piñon and cedar wood for the corner fireplaces in the houses, for the outdoor baking ovens, for the plaza bonfires. They are going for aspen poles to mend the fences of the night corral; for the trunks of pine trees, straight and sturdy, to replace vigas that have become warped with age; for willow, slender and supple, to make herringbone panels between the ceiling vigas of a new room that is to be added to a century-old house. At day's end they return, bringing wood and logs and willows, and long-needled pine boughs to roof an arbor which they later will build in the plaza facing the doors of the church.

This has been the first day of man-work in preparation for the yearly feast held on the pueblo's name day, the feast day of the patron saint of the village.

When the Spanish Padres, more than three hundred years ago, christianized the people of the pueblos and instructed them in the ways of the Spanish faith, the people built churches in the main plaza of each village. The first Mass celebrated in the new church was in honor of the saint whose feast day it happened to be, and the pueblo was given the name of this saint, in addition to its ancient Indian name. So it is that each year the pueblo holds a Spanish fiesta for a Christian saint, given in typical Indian fashion. To church ritual and Spanish merrymaking are added traditional Indian ceremonials.

In the pueblo, as Sun Father slowly moves toward its mid-morning place in the sky, the women begin the first day of woman-work. Young girls work with their mothers and grandmothers. Small boys, who this year are too young to go to the mountains with their fathers, carry baskets of white clay, finely ground powder, and buckets of water brought from the river to the doors of all the houses. In wooden troughs the Pueblo Old Mothers mix the water and clay to the right thickness and smoothness for whitewashing the walls. They are unerring in mixing the right consistency each time, and they have pride in the years it has taken to attain this perfection. The younger women watch with admiration and respect and await the time when they will be the Old Mothers and mix the clay for whitewashing.

On the sunny side of the house walls sit the Pueblo Old Fathers, whose eyesight and strength have been spent in the years that now lie behind them. But this morning they do not sit in idleness or neglect, bypassed by those who are still young and strong. Their place is important in today's work pattern. They are tending the babies and the toddlers and the next in size, telling them the legends of their Ancients. The young are quiet, attentive; even the bright-eyed babies peering out from their grandfathers' blankets are enfolded in the gentle, loving voices of the Old Ones. It is on such days and in such a manner that the ways of the Ancients enter into the minds and the hearts of the young and become part of the subconscious of those who tomorrow will place their feet into the larger, older footprints that have made yesterday's trail deep and straight.

The younger women have their place, also, preparing for the coming fiesta. Their first task is to replaster all the rooms of the houses. They take the clay mixture the Old Mothers have made ready for them and, standing on boxes, chairs, and ladders, with mitts of rabbit fur, pat and smooth it on the walls. At the base of the walls they make a "baby-high border" of yellow-brown clay flecked with mica. In making these borders, they use no measuring sticks or markers, only their eyes, yet the border runs a straight line, neither wavering nor blotched, around the four sides of the rooms. This clay is used as trim and for the inside of fireplaces and the niches where the wooden statues of the saints—centuries-old family treasures—are kept from generation to generation. Before the saints are returned to their freshly plastered niches, they are repainted and decorated with new clothing and fresh paper flowers. New candles are dipped for the tin candleholders that hang beside the statues on the wall.

Navajo blankets, woolen shawls, silk lace-edged shoulder kerchiefs, deerskins, woven mantas, feather headdresses, and beaded leggings are aired in the bright November sunshine and then replaced on the pole-for-the-soft-things that hangs from the vigas by rawhide thongs. Bracelets, arm bands, and necklaces of silver, coral, and shell are rearranged on the pole-for-the-hard-things on the opposite wall. The cupboard and the straight-back chairs are repainted. New oilcloth is bought for the long, narrow table where food is served. The earthen floors are soaked with a mixture of oxblood saturated with salt and, when dry, are polished by women using the small handstones that have been handed down to them by the grandmothers of their grandmothers. At last all the rooms of all the houses are ready for Fiesta. But this is only the beginning.

Now the women turn to out-of-doors work. The outside house walls are plastered with mud, sand-brown in color, as is the earth that holds them. The squat chimneys are topped with new clay pots, their bottoms broken to fit the chimneys. The doors and window frames are painted "Virgin Mary" blue. The beehive-shaped adobe ovens are replastered and in them short pieces of wood are laid, ready for firing.

Then, like a hive of bees swarming, the women alight on the church, on its roof, its walls, inside and outside. Every inch is replastered, repainted, or polished. The statues are dressed in new robes of silk and velvet. The age-old patron saint gets a completely new wardrobe. The altar linens and vestments are washed and ironed and mended. New candles are dipped for the candle-holders on the walls and the altar. New paper flowers are made to place in stiff bouquets before the statues of the saints.

The plaza is swept, sprinkled with water, and swept again until the clean, hard earth glows like waxed old wood, polished not by hand but by centuries of bare feet that have walked its length and breadth.

The men cut and saw the firewood they have brought down from the mountains. They repair roofs and fences and perhaps build a new room for some family that has outgrown its small house on the plaza. They build an arbor where the statue of their patron saint will be enthroned on the feast day. The arbor roof is heavy with pine boughs and the floor is covered with pine needles. When the arbor is finished, the women line it with their choicest shawls, their most treasured kerchiefs. Tall tin candlesticks hold, as they have for centuries, hand-dipped candles ready for lighting.

Now come the days for the preparation of the food that will be needed, not only for the people of the village but for Indian relatives and friends who will come from many miles away. Food will not be served to the non-Indian visitors. The people of the pueblo will be much too busy honoring their saint to cater to the wants and needs of strangers. Counting themselves and Indian visitors staying with them, there may be several hundred to feed. This food must be prepared beforehand since there will be no time for cooking on the great day and the eve before it.

Beef and mutton are butchered and cut into hunks for roasting and into strips for boiling. Corn, beans, chili, and onions are stewed with bite-size pieces of meat in earthenware pots over fireplace coals. Tortillas of blue and yellow corn are baked on tins and rolled in cloth-tied bundles, to be eaten cold when needed. *Biscochitos* (little sweet cakes) and half moons of fried pies filled with ground piñon nuts, meat, and raisins are stored away. The wood in the adobe ovens is burned to ashes, then raked out, and loaves of wheat-flour bread put in to bake.

Fiesta clothes are cleaned and mended. Deerskin moccasins and leggings are whitened. Hair is washed in suds made of pounded yucca roots and rinsed in juniper berry water. The pueblo and the people are ready for Fiesta.

Now thoughts are turned to those who will participate in the traditional ritual for celebration. What dance ceremonial will be given? Who will the dancers be?

On a certain year it is decided that the dance ceremonial will be the eagle dance. The young men who
are selected to give the dance go to the kiva for a four-
day retreat, staying in the cold ceremonial room
without fire of any kind and eating but one ear of yellow corn a day. They say the traditional prayers, perform the traditional rituals. They cleanse their minds
and hearts and bodies of human desires.

On the day of the dance they will have become one
with their brothers, the eagles, soaring in flight on the
crest of the wind, unmindful that, since they are men,
their feet are tied to the ground. On the day of the
dance, the people watching them will see, not their sons
or brothers, but giant eagles condescending to be earth-
bound for their red-skinned brothers' Christian feast
day.

The time of preparation is over. All is ready. Tomorrow will be Fiesta Eve.

* * * * *

Fiesta Eve

Sun Father, a glowing disc in a scarlet sky, rises slowly
over the mountains. The morning air is thin and still,

clear and cold. Midday warms, with snow clouds hiding the mountains and the foothills. On this Fiesta Eve, snow begins falling fitfully—a flurry of snow, a flash of sunshine, a gust of wind, a flurry of snow.

Indian guests dribble into the plaza, mostly Pueblo Indians from villages to the north and west, but also a few Navajo, a few Apache. They come by automobile, in trucks and wagons, on horseback, afoot. Cars and trucks are parked in the shelter of house walls, their motors blanketed against the threat of a freezing night. Wagons are abandoned out of sight of the plaza. No vehicles of any kind are there. Harnesses and saddles, saddle blankets, and bridles are stored in the houses where the guests are visiting. Horses are put in the night corral and fed grain and hay in generous amounts from the scanty supply of the host pueblo.

This is the beginning of Fiesta. The plaza is filled with a babble of tongues—Tewa, Tigua, Keresan, Shoshone, Apache, Navajo, English, Spanish—as each guest is welcomed into the household inviting him, and warmth and food are offered.

Snow stops falling and the hours of afternoon pass swiftly. Day's ending comes quickly and as quickly passes. The setting sun has but a moment of brilliance, turning for a breath of time the snow-rimmed peaks of the Sangre de Cristos as red as the blood of the dying Christ, the blood that gives this mountain range its name.

Smoke, scented with the spices of burning piñon and cedar wood, curls upward from the chimneys of the houses. Through house windows lamplight sends a warm yellow glow into the gathering shadows of evening. As Sun Father takes his warmth from the land, cold creeps down the mountains, through the low-lying foothills, and across the valley. Before morning, the slow-running water in the shallow river bed will be crusted with a thin sheet of ice and the water-heavy snow in the road ruts will be icy slush.

In the plaza, dark-blanketed men move silently, doing the tasks that they have been given the privilege of doing. At each end of the plaza, seemingly at exactly the same second, two great fires are kindled to crackling flames of red and gold, leaping upward, higher and higher, as if to touch the first stars of evening. Someone opens wide the heavy, hand-carved doors of the old church that has stood rooted deep in the earth of the plaza for more than two hundred years. One by one the candles in the church are lighted. Someone pulls the bell ropes and the church bells clang out, making a trail of sound through the open doors of the church to the closed doors of the houses. Abruptly the clanging stops. There is no echo, only the remembered sound.

As if by a signal, house doors open. Men, women, children come into the plaza and walk across its emptiness to the church. The Old Ones do not lag. The

younger people do not hurry. Boys do not run or shove
or try to trip each other. Young girls do not loiter, con-
fiding secrets with whispered laughter. Old and young
walk with stately measured tread. They walk with dig-

nity. The old church fills with people, its Indian people, who built it by the labor of their hands, molding the sun-dried bricks for its thick walls, hewing the giant vigas for its roof beams, carving the great doors, the altar, the Stations of the Cross, and the statue of their saint. The old church fills; men kneel on one side, opposite the women. Children sit on the floor as close as possible to the haven of their mothers' shawls. Babies on their mothers' backs look wide-eyed at the flickering candles. Dogs creep stealthily into the shadowy corners for warmth and sleep. The altar boy swings the heavy incense burner with all his small strength, and the musty smell of its smoke blends with the musty smell of damp adobe walls.

Tomorrow the Padre will come to the pueblo from the cathedral in Santa Fe to celebrate Fiesta Mass, but tonight belongs wholly to the Indians. The Pueblo sacristan leads his people in prayers. The prayers are long ones. They go on and on and on while candles drip and babies reluctantly give themselves to sleep, and at last they end. The kneeling men and women stand; children are collected; babies are shrugged into comfortable positions on their mothers' backs; dogs are shooed from the church, howling in protest. With careful reverence the saint, splendid in his new attire, is placed on a satin-covered litter under a crimson canopy deeply fringed with gold. The people crowd back against the walls, making a wide aisle down the center of the church, so those who are carrying the litter may go into the plaza to lead them in procession.

Joyfully the church bells ring and young men fire their guns into the air. Old men walking together chant in unison an ancient prayer. Old women mumble the prayers of the rosary, each one according to the way she has said them all the years since she was young. The middle-aged men and women and the older children sing hymns their Padres taught centuries ago, yesterday, and all the days and the years in between. The plaza fires, the window lamps, and the stars light the way of the people as they walk around the plaza and again around it and back into the church.

The saint is put in his place by the altar to rest until dawn of Fiesta morning. The people leave the church as quietly as they had entered it and at once become lost in the dark of the plaza passageways. The church bells are stilled; the candles are snuffed; the doors are closed.

In the deserted plaza the two flaming fires have died to smoldering coals. The house windows are not glowing with lamplight now. They are squares of darkness. The house doors are shut. The houses are empty of people. The entire village is enfolded in stillness, but not in the stillness of sleep. This is not a night for sleeping. This is the Eve of the Fiesta.

Deep in the darkness of the night, an Indian drum is heard—pounding, pounding, pounding. From the

edges of the village, other sounds drift in. In the night
corral the horses mill, well-fed and content. Under the
wagons, dogs snarl, seeking warmer places. In the
foothills, coyotes bark in mocking, derisive laughter. A
before-dawn whispers among the dried stubble in the
fields.

In the place to which the people have withdrawn,
an Indian drummer slaps his drum with the flat of his
hand and with each slap one sound rolls forth, deep,
rounded, complete. It throbs in the thick air of the ceremonial room. It throbs deep in the earth beneath the
drummer's feet and becomes the pounding of the heart-
beats of Earth Mother, who holds in her arms her Indian
children.

The stars hang low. Slowly, night walks across the
land. Slowly, fiesta dawn approaches. The drumbeats
pound.

* * * * *

Day of Fiesta

In the dark hour before dawn, small sounds and small
activities herald the coming of day. Horses stamp and
neigh. A car motor coughs and sputters. A dog barks,

chasing a rabbit. Boys shout, running to the river to break the thin ice crusting the water and return, laughing, aglow with cold and pleasure; lugging the heavy buckets of water that will be needed for horses and for household use. Dogs wait expectantly at house doors for bits of breakfast tortillas that might be thrown out to them. The ashes of last night's plaza fires are raked away, leaving no trace of last night's leaping flames or smoldering coals. The church doors are opened.

With the first ray of sunrise, women go into the church, making it ready for the morning Mass. They go into the arbor to straighten the shawl-hangings, to rearrange the artificial flowers on the table, to smooth the pine needles on the ground beneath it. They go out into the plaza to sweep away all marks of last night's procession. Last night had been the beginning, but today is the climax of the busy weeks of preparation. Today is the fulfillment of the centuries of having held precious those things that the first Padres had given them. Today is the feast day of their patron saint, the Christian name day of their pueblo.

With the plaza's sweeping completed, there comes an interval of quiet. The people go inside their houses; they close the doors. Slowly the Sun Father rises and blesses the land with his light and warmth. Slowly the brilliant colors of the sunrise fuse together and fade. Day of Fiesta has arrived!

Suddenly, children run from the houses, across the

plaza, over the bridge, along the road. They have neither seen nor heard an automobile, but somehow they know that the Padre's small car is about to come chugging around the turn of the hill. They are waiting there to meet him, calling their greetings in Tewa, Spanish, and English. They run beside his car, in front of it, behind it—an excited, merry escort. The people, dressed for fiesta, join the children, adding their welcome, filling the small car with gifts from every household. The Padre's car moves forward slowly, carefully. At last the Padre reaches the back wall of the church, parks the car, and blesses the people. Proud, young altar boys walk beside him into the sacristy of the church, where he will don the vestments of Mass, and they will put on their red serving robes and stiffly starched, white cotton tunics.

Mass begins. There is no choir; there is no organ, but all the people sing. Led by their sacristan, they sing the Mass hymns and their voices fill the plaza and fade into the silence of the distant hills. The Padre intones the prayers of the Mass. The older people give the responses in Spanish, but the children say them in English. The languages blend in melodic sounds, and the Mass in its mystic beauty reaches its climax and ends with the blessing. The saint, as on fiesta eve, is carried twice around the plaza. All altar boys walk beside the men who carry it, and beside their Padre. They bear lighted candles as high as they are tall. Finally the statue is placed on the table-throne in the arbor.

Then from afar an Indian drum is heard, and a chorus of old men chanting. The sounds draw nearer, and through the passageway the chorus appears. With them are two Eagle Dancers, who dance first before the open doors of the church and then before the arbor that holds the statue of the saint.

The dancers, flanked by the chorus, stop at a point midway between the church and the arbor. The two Eagle Dancers are young men, about the same age and height. Their heads are covered with caps of raw cotton to which are attached large yellow-green eagle beaks. Their faces are yellow-green, with red blotches painted beneath their eyes. Their hands and arms and feet and legs are yellow-green. Their buckskin kilts are belted with turquoise and girdled with bells; small bells are tied beneath their knees with scarlet yarn. On their chests and backs are the downy feathers of eagles, and along their arms are widespread, sweeping eagle wings.

As they dance, the curve of their heads, their beaks, their bodies, and the curve of their wings cast on the ground the shadows of two soaring eagles ready for flight. Indians and non-Indians alike are fascinated by the spectacle of men who, having possessed themselves of the spirits of eagles, become eagles in every movement, in every line of their bodies.

The chorus of Old Ones, accompanied by drumbeat, rattle, and gourd, sing in syllables of sounds rather than words. The rhythm of their singing is completely dif-

ferent from the rhythm of the dancers. The two parts,
chorus and dance, are separate yet complement each
other in sound and beat.

When the dance is finished, dancers and chorus return to the kiva. After an interval, two new dancers perform. This pattern is repeated throughout the day. The dance teams alternate, but the appearance of the dancers, the dance steps, and the chorus remain the same.

Women are seen carrying food to the kiva. Between the dances the non-Indian visitors walk about, chat among themselves and with their Indian friends. The tourists look admiringly at the silver, turquoise, and coral ornaments the Indians wear, longing to buy them. They peer in house windows for a glimpse of clay jars, pots, and plates. They do not buy. Nothing is sold. Today is a festival and not a day for the transaction of business.

This fiesta day, snow begins falling—at first only a hint of snowflakes, but soon it falls softly, thickly, steadily. Gray snow clouds, soft as velvet, close the plaza in on every side. The non-Indian visitors leave hurriedly. Even the Indian guests begin to depart, reluctantly, yet fearful of the intensity of the coming storm. The people of the pueblo stand in groups as they have been standing since morning. The only notice of the storm they permit themselves to take is to draw more tightly into their shawls and blankets as they watch their Eagle Dancers perform an ancient ritual, which in all probability had been set in its pattern centuries before Christ was born. Snowflakes mingle with the downy feathers on the backs of the Eagle Dancers and with the raw cotton that covers their heads, but seemingly they neither feel nor see them. Snow falls on the kerchief-banded heads and the velvet blouses of the Old Ones in the chorus, but they are unmindful of its falling.

The dance keeps on until what would have been the time of sunset, if Sun Father could have pierced the snow clouds to shine through in crimson glory to climax the day. But at this moment, although there are no sunset colors to announce it, day comes to an end. Dancing stops.

Now dancers and chorus return to the kiva. There is no chanting, no thud of drum or rasping, grating of pebbles being shaken in sun-dried hollow gourds. The only sounds that can be heard are the sharp quick ones the rattles make on girded kilts and knee-ties as the dancers walk through the storm to the cold, darkening kiva.

There are no visitors left in the pueblo. The village is now as it was before fiesta. Snow clouds close out the world on the other side of the river as if such a world did not exist. The swirling snow muffles the noises of evening and blots out the block-shaped outlines of the houses. Snow piles deep in the plaza, drifts against house walls, tops the flat roofs. The ice in the river is snow-covered. The deep arroyos are snow-filled from bank to bank. The twisting lane, the sandy road, the bare fields lie under an unwrinkled blanket of white.

The people are alone again; fiesta has come and has gone. Tomorrow will be a new day, with new duties and new responsibilities having to do with the life of today as well as with the traditions of ancient rituals and the ceremonies of prayer.

Tired and happy, the people sleep. Snow keeps falling.

* * * * *

Time of Waiting

The snow storm of this fiesta is of short duration, being only the first hint of winter that late October or early November often brings to the highland country. By the following noontime, snow has stopped falling. A brilliant sun shines down on a world so glistening white it sparkles with myriad splintered iridescent stars.

By mid-week most of the snow has melted, leaving only patches of white on the shady sides of the sand dunes and rims of white topping the distant blue mountains. The dry, sandy soil drinks in the melting snow water, leaving only traces of dampness where snowdrifts have been. The thick adobe walls, drying in the warm sunshine, smell like freshly turned earth in the springtime, although real winter is but a new moon away.

In the Tewa village there is an interval of quiet. Communal activities have stopped. Only necessary daily chores are done, and these by individuals rather than by groups of people working together.

During the long nights, now that "the thunder sleeps," families gather around their hearth fires and listen to the Old Ones tell stories of the Ancients. Two Old Ones are absent. They are seen neither day nor night, but even the small ones know where they are and what they are doing. They are counting the days for their people.

Summer Chief and Winter Chief, each in his own place and each in his own way, count the days until Sun Father on his journey across the roof of the world will reach the Middle Place. Each chief watches the shadows as they pass over some special place—a jut of rock, a stump of tree, a mountain gap. Each chief watches the stars in their places in the night sky, as their Ancients have done since time began and have so ordained that it shall be done until the end of time. Each watches for signs that will tell him that the day has come for Sun-in-his-house-to-rest.

The people wait for solstice, but not yet are the counted days enough for this to happen. Not yet are the signs the correct ones. Not yet have the Winter Cloud People come. Solstice is nearing, but it has not arrived. So the people wait, patiently, calmly, knowing that all things come to pass in their own good time. The pueblo is a place of quiet.

At the government Indian day school built at the end of a twisting lane that seems to lead away from the pueblo rather than to it, this is not a quiet time. This is a busy time in preparation for the Day of Thanksgiving for non-Indian people.

Indian schoolchildren color paper cutouts of the Pilgrim Fathers and bring them home, small gifts for the Old Ones. They carefully explain, as their teachers have taught them, that Pilgrims are the Ancients of the white people, who have left the tradition of giving a ceremonial of thanks to their Giver-of-Life on one day of every year.

The Old Ones look at the cutouts, even more puzzled by the explanation than by the pictures of the Pilgrims. Only one day each year to give thanks to the Giver-of-Life for all that He has bestowed on his non-Indian children? They cannot understand—these Old Ones, who give the One-who-holds-their-life-trails a prayer of thanks at the completion of every act of every day. They finger the cutouts and look at them in silent disapproval. White ways may be good, but they are difficult to comprehend and to accept.

Sensing the unspoken rejection, the little Indians look at the cutouts they had brought home with such pride and at their loved and revered Old Ones. They, too, are puzzled and they are saddened, knowing without words, but deep in their hearts, how difficult it is to bridge two worlds.

At school the flurry of expectations continues. The

children color and cut pictures of Pilgrim mothers and log cabins, of turkeys and "the forest primeval," but their thoughts are at home with their people who are waiting for the Summer and the Winter Chiefs to tell them that Sun Father rests in his house and all is well with their world.

The days of the November month slip by.

❖ ❖ ❖ ❖ ❖

Time of Solstice

The month of December comes to the Tewa country with days bright and clear and warm, and nights bright and clear and freezing cold. The cloudless sky of day is infinite blue upon blue; the night sky is a velvet black star-design blanket covering the Pueblo world and hanging so low that it can almost be touched by the fingertips.

The Winter Cloud People come. How they come, for what purpose, and in what manner their coming is received by the Indians is not shared with non-Indian neighbors. During this time the pueblo closes in upon itself. It becomes impenetrable, aloof, holding close its people and its secrets.

Days pass and more days pass. At last Sun Father stands at the solstice place. At sunrise the War Captain, wrapped in his blanket, appears on the topmost roof of the terraced houses, a dark silhouette against the sky. His high voice rises and falls in rhythmic cadence, telling the people that the retreat of the Summer Chief and the Winter Chief is ended and now begins the retreat of the people. For four days and four nights they are housebound. Nothing is to be taken into their houses: no food, no water, no firewood. Nothing is to be taken from their houses: no ashes, no garbage, no refuse of any kind. In the plaza there must be no sound of voices. There must be neither fires nor the smoke of fires. The Sun in his house is resting, and likewise rest the children of the Sun.

The call is finished. The War Captain disappears. Echoes from the distant mountain linger in the thin morning air. "The Sun ... in his house ... rests ... rests."

At dawn of the fifth day, the pueblo comes alive. Houses are cleaned. The plaza is swept. All litter is placed at the edges of the village so Old Mother Wind may blow away the leavings of the summer season that now has departed. Solstice has come. It is now winter in the Tewa world.

Beginning of Long-Winter

The first two weeks of the December month pass by in days of golden sunshine. The Tewa world is a kaleidoscope of colors. The blue and purple mountains rise in stages from flat brown fields to yellow-gray sand dunes to green-blue foothills. Each rounded landswell bears its own color, distinct and separate—brown, yellow, green, blue, purple. Even the air has a quality of color: dazzling gold in daytime, freezing blue at night. It seems as if Earth Mother indulges herself in a last color-flaunting of joyous exuberance before being enfolded in the white mantle of long-winter.

Tewa women walk to the town market each day, carrying huge flour-sack-wrapped bundles. In the centuries-old Royal City of Santa Fe, they sit on the worn flagstones of the ancient palace portal and spread out on bright squares of calico the wares they have brought to town to sell. With soft laughter and song-sounding sentences in Tewa, they place saucy, jaunty, life-like little pottery animals in the center of each display and ring them in with corn necklace strings dyed in unbelievable colors, a last laugh at autumn. The little clay animals inside their rainbow fences of corn necklaces invite all passers-by to laugh with them at the whimsical skill of their Indian makers. As well as the small figures, there are large, beautiful jars, dough bowls and plates, each one molded or coiled, shaped, slipped, and fired according to its Pueblo type, but decorated by the potter who made it, with her special designs. These designs belong only to her or to a beloved granddaughter to whom she may leave them. For sale, also, are sand-cast silver and turquoise rings, earrings, and bracelets, and lovely strings of shell, coral, silver, and turquoise.

The men go to town each day with the women of their family. There is no work to be done in the pueblo in this time before real winter comes to stay. So they go to town and sit patiently by the squares of calico, or walk at the edges of the crowd and do a bit of trading with townspeople, winter visitors, or Indians from neighboring pueblos.

In the late afternoon they trudge the long miles back to their villages, carrying brown paper bags of store-bought groceries, pleased with market-day happenings but anxious to get home to the hearth fire before the night chill freezes the land.

Suddenly this carnival of colors ends. Between an evening and a morning, real winter comes, heralded by savage winds, swift and strong, that push against house walls with a million fingers, howl in fury, and are filled to bursting with thick, falling snow, powdery fine.

The Indians are overjoyed. Long-winter is here and its days and its work are upon them. The men make ready for the first deer hunt of winter. The horses are fed, bridled, and blanketed. In mid-morning the men ride them into the heart of the storm.

High above the Tewa world, held in the hand of a mountain, is a meadow guarded by towering peaks and jagged cliffs, sheltered by tall pines and slender aspen. In the heart of the meadow is a blue-green jewel whose brilliance changes with the changing light of day and season, but neither fades nor dims—the Sacred Lake of the Tewa. On the snow-covered banks of Sacred Lake, buck deer and doe and fawn leap and frolic, darting in and out among the sheltering trees, leaving small, heart-shaped tracks that the falling snow only partly erases.

Back in the pueblo, the women wait for the return of the hunters. The wind quiets. Snow stops falling. The sun shines down on a still, white world. Two days pass. The hunters do not come, but no one worries. The third day comes and near its end a call is heard. The women and children rush to the bridge to welcome the hunters and to learn how successful the hunt has been. Across the back of the lead horse is slung the carcass of a six-point buck; the second horse carries a buck deer, as does the third horse. No one speaks, but a sound soft as the sigh of the wind in the willows rustles among the waiting women as they follow their men to the plaza.

Blankets are brought from the houses and put on top of the hard-crusted snow in the plaza. Carefully, tenderly, in hushed and reverent silence, the deer are placed on the blankets. Sacred corn meal is brought from its keeping place. Carefully, tenderly, in hushed and reverent silence the deer are sprinkled and their parts are marked in accordance with the ancient ritual of sprinkling and marking. A long, melodic prayer is begun. The prayer reminds the deer that, in the other world before they came into this one, deer and men were brothers, and so they remain, forever bound together with the strong bonds of brotherhood.

The prayer goes on and on. A cold night wind chills the breath of the living as the death-wind has stilled the breath of the deer.

The prayer grows stronger, more vibrant, as it thanks the deer for permitting themselves to be sacrificed for the good, for the welfare, for the continuing life of their brothers, the Indians. At last the prayer ends in a moment of spiritual fraternal communion between man and his little brothers, the deer.

Pine flares are lighted to penetrate the shadows of descending night. The people work silently, swiftly, expertly. Now that the deer have been blessed and thanked, they are skinned and their parts portioned out to the people. The meat will be dried into strips of jerky and cooked in stews. The brains will be used in tanning the hides, making them into deerskin, soft and

45

pliable. The horns and hooves will be put away for future use. The ribs will be cleaned and allowed to dry and later used as instruments of rhythm in some sacred dance ceremonial.

Everything must be used. The deer, having sacri-

ficed life, must be made to know that the life they gave
has been received into a continuing life stream. Nothing
is wasted, not even the blood, which has been drained
into a bowl and placed where all can see it. The mothers
carry their boy babies into the plaza, where the bowl of

blood has been placed. They dip their fingertips into its holiness and mark their babies' feet and hands and foreheads, asking the spirits of the deer to give to their small ones the strength and the swiftness of deer, the grace and the gentleness.

The pine flares sputter and spark. The wind cries in the dry branches of the cottonwood trees. A pale moon shines down on a white-blanketed land. The Indians are shadow figures in an unreal world.

From the distant mountains comes a whispering echo like a whispered pounding of running feet. The Indians listen. They stop whatever they are doing and listen. It comes again, a mere ghost sound of the thud of running feet. The listening Indians smile. They understand what the echo tells them. The spirits of their brothers, the deer, have been released and are free.

Their work of tonight has been well done. At peace with all creatures, animal and man, the tired Indians go into their houses. The first deer hunt is only the beginning of the work of long-winter.

* * * * *

Christmas

All the Rio Grande Pueblo language groups, Tigua, Tewa, Keres, and Jemez, celebrate the week of Christmas with dance ceremonials. Most of these dances are traditional and part of a healing or some other ceremony, but some are given only for entertainment, mimicking the foibles of Indian and non-Indian, and dances borrowed from other tribes.

On the day before Christmas, the women and girls clean and decorate the church. For decoration they use great branches of mistletoe glistening with tiny seed-pearl berries, heavy boughs of evergreen still holding small, sweet-smelling pine cones, lacy cedar branches with beautiful bright-blue berries. The men have brought these gifts down to the pueblo from the mountains and piled them in heaps before the doors of the church.

Near the altar, the men build the crèche with pine boughs and cover its floor with straw. The wooden figures of the Holy Family, kept and treasured since the church was built and now repainted and dressed in new robes, are tenderly placed in the pine-bough shelter. The women bring their best clay animals, the ones they thought too good to sell, and group them in the straw beside the Holy Child's manger crib.

The women and girls scrape the dirty, half-frozen snow from the plaza and sweep it until it's as clean as the floors of their homes. When they have finished, if the Buffalo Dance is to be given, the men plant small pine trees in the center of the plaza, making it into a miniature forest. The boys build little towers of crisscross cedar sticks before all the doors facing the plaza.

49

They fill paper bags half full of sand, put candles (*farolitos*) in them, and place them near the edges of the house roofs, to be lighted at night.

With the first star of Christmas Eve the lamps in house windows, the candles in the church, and the *farolitos* on the rooftops are lighted. The luminaries of cedar sticks are kindled. The soft glow of lamps and candles and the flickering flames of the tiny fires give the plaza with its backdrop of houses a dramatic, theatrical appearance like an empty stage waiting the coming of the actors.

This Christmas Eve a Keres village on the banks of the Rio Grande is ready for the celebration of the birth of the Christian Holy Child. House doors open and shawled and blanketed figures come out and walk across the plaza to the church. They wander in and out of the church, kneel before the crèche to kiss the feet of the Santo Niño, to leave Him gifts, to say a prayer asking His blessing.

Shortly before the midnight hour, the Padre comes. Church bells ring; guns are fired. People crowd into the church to hear Mass and receive Holy Communion. The Mass ends and the Padre leaves, but the people stay. No one leaves the church or comes into the church. No one moves about or talks or prays. They wait.

Now is the time for the dancers to come into the church, to dance before the crèche, honoring the Holy

Infant with a prayer dance that was already patterned and set and old centuries before Christ's birth in the stable at Bethlehem. But tonight the dancers do not come. There is no muted sound of song or drum or gourd or rattle. Inside the church and outside in the pueblo there is only silence. Most silences in Indian villages are as serene, as peaceful as the deep, still waters of a mountain lake, but not this silence. This silence seems to quiver, heavy with the Indians' anxiety.

A freezing winter-night wind seeps through the thick walls of the old church. The Indians appear not to mind the intensity of the cold, but the non-Indian visitors suffer. The icy fingers of the below-zero temperature pierce through their clothes, making them ache unbearably. They are cold, stiff, miserable, and long to leave for the comparative comfort of their heated cars, but they do not go, unable to force themselves to walk through the crowd of kneeling Indians. Hours pass. The night wind stills, but the cold does not lessen. One hour, two hours, three hours drag by.

Suddenly the silence is broken. The Indians rise from their knees to stand against the walls, clearing a place before the altar and the crèche. The church doors are opened and the morning star shines in upon the Babe in the manger.

There has been, apparently, no word spoken, no message received, no visible communication of any kind, and yet Indians and non-Indians know that the waiting is over. They know that anxiety is gone and that joy has taken its place. They know the reason for the waiting, for the anxiety, and now for the joy. Through the hours of the night this Christmas Eve, through the silence and the cold, a young mother of the Keres people was awaiting the birth of her first child. With her, the people and the dancers waited. Now the child is born. An Indian child is born on the night of the birth of the Christ child. A son is born on this holy night, a boy of the Keres people.

Now song, drumbeat, rattle, and gourd cut through the cold. The old drummer comes first, and behind him the chorus, ten men in two lines, to stand by the crèche, singing the dancers into the place cleared for them. Heading the dancers are two buffalo figures carrying poles tied with eagle feathers, the dance banners of the Buffalo Dance. Thirty dancers, men and women, follow them and the dance begins. It continues on into Christmas morning.

* * * * *

Day of the Election of Officers

Christmas dances end on the last night of December. Early in the morning of January 1, all the small boys go from house to house receiving gifts of bread, but the bread is not a treat for them, nor is the day one of merrymaking and gaiety. All day the pueblo has a deserted look. Visitors do not come; there would be no one to receive them. A few children play in the plaza, but their play is hushed. The women remain indoors. The men are at meeting.

This is the day of the election of officers for the coming year—governor, lieutenant governor, the *principales* who will make up the council, and the War Captain, who is the emissary of the Cacique to his people.

The Cacique, spiritual head and absolute authority in the affairs of the pueblo, names the men who hold the right to be elected for office. The heads of the families of the village elect them, not by a majority but unanimously. There must be no dissension. Each man gives his views in a serious, quiet, lengthy manner. Each viewpoint is discussed, weighed, and at last accepted or rejected by everyone. This takes all day and far into the night. The offices are civil ones and have no religious significance, but the selection of the men who will hold them is attended to in a serious and formal manner because of their importance and the dignity which surrounds the offices. The men who hold them must do so in humility and with full realization that they hold positions of trust. It is the offices that are honored, not the men who hold them, for Pueblo people do not recognize individual greatness. Even the Cacique is looked upon as only a spokesman, a liaison between his people, men of earth, and the Unseen Power.

When at last the officers are elected, there are no congratulations. There is, instead, prayer that each man may fulfill his obligations in accordance with the plan of the Ancients for the People's good and in as much harmony as possible with the government of the non-Indian people.

At the meeting's end the man who has been elected Governor receives two canes. The older one was given the Indians by the early Spanish government. The other is called the Lincoln Cane because it was given them by Abraham Lincoln. Almost a hundred years ago, the Pueblo governors made the long journey to Washington, D.C., to receive from President Lincoln a silver-headed cane inscribed with the name of the pueblo and "A. Lincoln, President 1873." This is the Governor's badge of office.

Each year since then, the two canes have had a prominent place in the main room of the house of the Governor. Nothing must ever harm the canes. Though the pueblo may be swept by epidemics, drought, flood, or fire, the canes must be kept safe and unscarred. Every child knows this. The Governor's children know that, the year the canes are in the keeping of their father, this in no way adds to their greatness, only to their responsibility.

* * * * *

Epiphany

The week before the feast of Epiphany, the Christian feast day that commemorates the visit of the Three Kings to the Infant Jesus, is a busy one. Each of the newly elected officers will give a feast in his home on that day. The wives of the new officers hurry their pottery-making; by mid-week they are ready for market and walk the long miles to town with their wares. When they return at nightfall, each dollar brought by sales has been spent for lard, flour and other food for feasting on Three Kings' Day. The rest of the week is spent in cooking.

On this day of January 6, the men who were elected to office on New Year's accept the public recognition of their office. But they are not acclaimed and feted by their townsmen; rather, they are the ones who must give the feast. The elected pay tribute to those who permit them to serve.

Feasting begins early in the morning at each of the houses in which an officer lives. There is no precedent in serving. One does not start at the Governor's table and continue from house to house, ending at the feast table of the officer who is keeper of the keys of the church. Food is served at the same time at all the houses. Each member of the pueblo, out of natural courtesy, sees to it that no one house is crowded while another table remains empty. Food is the same at each house. If one man can afford more than his neighbor, it would be unbecoming to his office to show it by serving better food. The feast consists of corn, meat and chili stews, beans, oven bread, macaroni and cheese, bread pudding, Jello, and coffee. Every Indian and non-Indian must eat at every house. It takes a great quantity of food to serve several hundred people, for not only do the townsmen feast, but also non-Indians, who come from all the nearby towns.

In the afternoon there is a dance ceremonial. There may be a church christening for some child fortunate enough to have been born near Three Kings' Day. Such a child is given for his or her baptismal name Rey or Reyecita, the Spanish form of "king." At this time the family gives presents to friends, according to what it can afford to give.

January slips by in snow and sunshine. Snow lies in shallow, windswept drifts in the shade of house walls and melts in patches of dampness out in the sunshine. The Sangre de Cristos are blue-misted in morning and red-crowned at sunset. Water flows under the ice in all the rivers.

* * * * *

Ceremonials of Long-Winter

Long-winter is at its peak. The short January days are softened by falling snow or whipped by freezing wind, and warmed only briefly by the sunshine of midday. In every pueblo, on almost every day of this month of winter, some dance ceremonial is given. On almost every evening, children's dance groups go from house to house practicing the dances they are being trained to give. No child who has learned to walk is considered too young to dance, and many a long line of fifty dancers ends with a group of three-year-olds mimicking the dance step and body posture of the older dancers in front of them.

In the Days of the Old at long-winter, when the foods of the harvest—the vegetables and the grains, the fruits and the berries, the roots and the nuts that had been stored for winter use—had been eaten, the storerooms were empty. Since it was winter, once the stored harvest had been consumed, the Indians' hunger could no longer be satisfied by the plant foods of the land, so it had to be met by the food that the animals of the land could provide. Therefore, the Indian, represented by his Hunt Society, petitioned the buffalo and the deer, the elk and the antelope to give themselves to fulfill his needs, and he honored them by impersonation and ceremony.

Thus it was in the Days of the Old, and today these same ceremonies are given. Little has been taken from them or added to them since they were first given, centuries ago.

Each pueblo has its own interpretation of the dance ceremonial, its own manner of costuming for the animal impersonations, its own chants, tempo, and form of presentation. Aside from these differences, the winter dances have much in common. They have a chorus of chanters, a dance leader, a mother-spirit, huntsmen, and animal figures. They have a common purpose: to appease the spirit of the animals, thus luring them to capture.

During these winter dances, members of the Society of Fun Makers perform, to the delight of onlookers but unnoticed by the dancing group. The Fun Makers are known by different names in the different language groups—chiffonati among the Tigua, kossa in the Tewa villages, and koshare in the Keres pueblos. The Fun Makers are members of a curing society who also have control of rain and floods. Sometimes members inherit their place in the society; others are recruited after having been "cured" or "captured" by a magic rite.

The purpose of the Fun Makers is to bring laughter, and their power is considered so great that they may say what they choose and do what they want. They may mimic and ridicule anything, no matter how important or sacred it happens to be. At intervals between the dances, and also while the men are dancing, they run up and down ladders, in and out of houses, among people watching the dancers, and often into the midst of the dance itself, to capture some small dancer until his cries bring rescue.

The Fun Makers wear no masks, but their faces are painted in grotesque designs, and in most of the villages their bodies are painted in stripes of black and white or black and yellow. Occasionally they are painted pink or gray from minerals found at the pueblo's Sacred Lake. They wear corn husks in their hair.

There are other ceremonials held in long-winter besides the prayer-petitions of the Hunt Society to the game animals. Since Indians fought other tribes only for the use of the game trails and never for the possession of land, war dances of long-winter are also petitions for continuing food supply.

Other rituals are given at this time by the society having control of winter storms. These are invocations that snow may fall frequently and heavily in the high places, filling the deep, rock-walled canyons so that the warmth of spring may fill the mountain lakes and mountain streams with melted snow water. The lakes and streams then will fill the irrigation ditches, to bring water to summer crops.

✿ ✿ ✿ ✿ ✿

Tigua Deer Dance

Near the northern boundary of New Mexico, almost at the source of the Rio Grande, in a fertile valley at the foot of towering mountains stands Taos of the Tigua people. Tallest-terraced and most majestic of all the pueblos, it consists of two great houses divided by a little stream but united by common blood and tongue and ways into one people, one pueblo.

During a summer sunrise, as one stands in the plaza below, the terraces of Taos delight the eye. Each terrace, with its row of houses teeming with people, children, dogs and cats, birds in wicker cages, flowers abloom in pots, lines of bright scarlet chili, dull-red jerky, and bunches and "ladders" of ears of colored corn, seems like one busy street placed above the other.

On a summer noontime, the pueblo is hushed and still. The Tigua are having siesta, resting in the shade of house walls that hem in the many tiny, hidden, flower-filled patios. The children are sleeping. The birds in their cages are quiet. The cats and the dogs are napping.

On a summer evening the clear cool mountain air

60

is filled with song as the Tigua young men wrapped in their white cotton blankets stand on the bridge of the trickling stream, singing love songs to the Tigua young women. Safe inside their houses, the women listen to the notes of the flutes and the words of the songs and can picture the dark handsome young men in their white blankets, singing in the mountain moonlight.

But now it is winter, a winter dawn heavy and brooding and gray. Men walk across the plazas to the kiva, speak to the kiva guard, and climb down the ladder to the ceremonial room, dug deep into the earth. This is a January day in long-winter, a day when the Tigua people give their Dance for the Deer.

The fields of Taos lie hidden under a blanket of snow. The snow-rimmed mountains seem so close to the edge of the village that a reaching hand could touch their rock ledges and deep-shadowed canyons and purple peaks.

Shortly after dawn, Taos women begin the work of the day, when the dancers must be feasted and the chiffonati (Fun Makers) given gifts of bread. They go to the river for water. They sweep the terraces and the patios and plazas. They build the cook fires in the fireplaces in the houses and in the ovens on the terraces. Among the women, there is the soft hum of talk and laughter. But children do not go outside to play, and the only men seen walking across the plaza are carrying their kiva bundles down into the ceremonial room.

The War Captain gives the call for the people to come to the church. Three times he gives the call; the church bells ring, and the sound of call and bell echoes from the distant peaks. Work stops. Before the echoes have died away, white-blanketed men and boys walk across the plaza. Black-shawled women and girls, whose bright full skirts show an edge of color between the blackness of the shawls and the whiteness of their wide, high, deerskin boots, walk across the plaza. The church is filled. The Tigua pray, asking the Christian God to bless the day of dancing for the deer. Prayer completed, they hurry back to whatever tasks they had been doing when the crier's voice was heard. Only the men who are not dancing return to their houses. All others are in the kiva, where rooftop is level with the hard, tramped earth of the plaza. Only the ladder poles and the kiva guard make known to the non-Indian visitor to pass by and quickly, for this place is the holy place of the Taos people, and no other people are welcome here.

The sun pierces the snow clouds, and Tigua and visitors begin drifting into the plaza to wait for the dancers.

About midday, distant cries are heard, strange, weird-sounding cries, unlike those that are made by men. All eyes are turned toward an adobe wall from where the cries have come, and above the wall top are seen the antlers of the advancing deer. The long line moves slowly beyond the wall and finally around its end into the plaza. The dancers move forward with hesitation, as if reluctant to come, and yet mindful of the need that awaits them—a long line of probably fifty men and boys, each one wrapped full length in the hides of deer, their only other clothing being dark kilts and low, brown deerskin moccasins. The heads of the deer hang forward, almost covering the faces of the dancers. The only color is the sand-brown and brown-white of the deer hides and the deeper brown of the dancers' bodies.

The line is led by the spirit-mother of the deer. She is dressed in a white deerskin robe and wears the high, wide, white deerskin boots. Her black, shining hair is loose and at the top is tied with a single downy eagle feather. In one hand she carries a sprig of evergreen, and in the other a gourd rattle. The deer-men form a long, dancing line. At certain times in the dance they stop dancing and the woman moves slowly down the line and back again. She gestures with the gourd; they kneel. She reverses her steps and gestures, and the men rise and dance again. The chiffonati provide the laughter, and the dance moves on until day's end, when they return to the kiva.

The Taos Deer Dance is neither colorful nor dramatic, but it is the best example of the Rio Grande winter dances of unchanged, earliest primitive art form, where the masks are the preserved animal skins undecorated by abstract design.

*****

Tewa Deer Dance

Down the great River of the North from Taos is a Tewa pueblo of scattered, one-story houses, in appearance much like the nearby towns of their Spanish-American neighbors. However, in this village, instead of a flat-roofed, white-walled church, typical of both pueblos and Spanish towns, there is a steepled stone one, replica of a church in France that many years ago a Padre living and working in the New World, yet homesick for France and the town of his boyhood, had built in the sandhills of the Rio Grande.

During long-winter the Deer Dance is given in this village, as in all the Rio Grande pueblos, but there is little similarity between this Tewa dance and the one given by the Tigua. The purpose and the organization of the dance are the same, and the dates often coincide. But the costumes of the dancers are different, and so is the "atmosphere" of the dance.

The Tewa deer are much more stylized and less deer-like. The dancer's face is completely in view and, although not masked, is painted. The deer antlers he wears are attached to a tight-fitting buckskin cap, tied under his chin, and dotted with eagle down. Around his

head is a visor of thin yucca strips. His hair knot is ringed with cornhusks, and in it is a fan of eagle feathers. The dancer's costume is made up of a white cotton shirt, a white embroidered kilt, and white crocheted leggings, gathered at the knees with a string of bells. His moccasins are white deerskin with skunk-fur heelpieces. Instead of sticks to imitate the deer's forelegs, the Tewa dancer carries a long staff topped with evergreen and eagle feathers. He also carries a gourd rattle.

When a line of twenty or thirty of these dancers comes into the plaza, there is a breath of silence among the onlookers in delight at the dramatic spectacle of virile, strong men dancing to honor the deer that give them so much. The dance steps of the Tewa dance are more pronounced, suggesting, not imitating, the grace of the deer. The movement in the long line of dancers is absolutely precise, but the stark realism and the primitive force of the Tigua dance are lacking. The Tewa dance has the quality of theater—dramatic, sophisticated—but when the Tigua deer come into the plaza of Taos, they are not men performing. They are wild creatures, hesitant, frightened, confused, yet compelled onward, by love for their Indian brothers, to offer themselves in sacrifice.

The Buffalo Dance is also a common winter dance among the Pueblo groups. Occasionally there are dances in which the dancers impersonate buffalo, deer,

elk, antelope, and mountain goat, the hunters who capture them, and the spirit-mother who is always with
them. These dances are great pageants given in
natural, outdoor settings, where each dancer plays his
individual part, fitting it into the smooth design of the
whole. The spirit-mother moves with the dignity and
pride of the woman-figure, holder of life. The stalking
hunters, the slow, lumbering buffalo, the shy deer, the
haughty elk, the frolicking antelope, and the mountain
goat are impersonated flawlessly in every gesture,
step, and movement of the dancers.

All these dances differ from group to group, but they
are part of the year cycle that the Rio Grande Pueblo
people have in common. They are as much a part of
life to these people as birth and death, planting and har-
vesting, hunger and the providing of food.

The non-Indian looks at these dances. The Indian
lives them.

* * * * *

Spring Waiting Time

February comes with its small promise of spring and
its flaunting threats of continued winter. Sun Father,

67

usually so generous with light and warmth, shines palely through thick clouds of dust.

Wind blows incessantly in clouds of stinging sand, laying flat the dried weeds of winter, tumbling the tumbleweeds across the snow-patched fields, pushing relentlessly against everything in its path, seeping through thick housewalls, and laying in waves of dust beneath the windows and under the cracks of the doors.

The pueblo plaza seems an unfriendly place, with wind swirls blowing drifts of sand and piles of tumbleweed against house walls. Doors remain closed. Indians are remote, withdrawn. Even the schoolchildren, generally responsive and loving, become as strangers to their teachers, beyond the point of reaching.

The dance ceremonials of long-winter that filled the pueblo plaza with color and movement, drumbeat and song, and gave to the non-Indian a sense of the unity of life—plant, animal, man—are finished. It is as if they had not been. The times the non-Indian has feasted at the Indian table, has sat before his hearth fire viewing the house dances of evening, listening far into the night to the Old Fathers' stories of the days of their Ancients, are now as if they had not been.

The non-Indian knows that he has not been a part of the rituals preceding the plaza dances. He has been permitted only to view their culmination, and yet, having viewed these, he had felt a closeness, a oneness in spirit with his Indian neighbor. This, now, is gone. The pueblo has turned in upon itself, not pushing aside neighbors and teachers, but simply unmindful of their existence.

This is the time of retreat for many of the traditional societies of the religious organization of the pueblo. This is the time for the counting and recording of the days. Since Christmas the Summer Chief and the Winter Chief have been watching the sunrise and the sunset, the sun shadows and the stars in the night sky. They have been noting the signs and the omens which announce the coming of solstice. This is, once again, the time of the seasonal transfer.

This is a time to be shared among themselves and their Indian Ancients and not with an alien outside world. This is a time sufficient, rounded, whole, complete to the Indian, who knows what it is all about, but to the non-Indian neighbor the month drags by.

Toward the month's ending there is change in the tempo and the mood of the people of the village. Once more the non-Indian is permitted to share in the seasonal activities. Once more he is allowed to feel kinship with his Indian brother.

Time of the Cleaning of the Ditches

The Summer Chief and the Winter Chief meet in the house of the Governor to discuss the cleaning of the mother ditch and all the feeder ditches. The discussion takes all day and into the night. Each man tells of the signs he has noted. They seem to be right. Each man talks of the appearance of the stars. They are of good omen. Each man tells of the days recorded. Their numbers tally. Finally it is decided that the time has come when the irrigation ditches are to be repaired and cleaned and blessed for the coming of the water to irrigate the crops that soon will be planted.

With the coming of sunrise, the War Captain cries out the news to the people. Tomorrow the men will clean the ditches. Today the women will prepare the food they will serve tomorrow. The people listen and laughter flows around the plaza as the water of mother ditch will flow when the gates are opened. The call of the work of tomorrow is an announcement of spring. Like the first robin, it brings tidings of the coming summer.

All day the women cook. They roast and bake and boil and fry enough food to last for the days of ditch-cleaning. All day they work and talk and laugh together. The men joke among themselves and tease the women. At school the children are excited. They are noisy. Their laughter floods the schoolroom like the melting snow water floods the valley at the foot of the mountains. The War Captain has called out the orders. Springtime is coming.

Before the next day's dawn has completely blotted out the darkness of night, the men, armed with hoes and shovels, set out for the day's work. The Old Fathers wear ceremonial deerskin leggings and moccasins. The younger men are content with blue-jeans, bright-colored shirts, store-bought shoes, red kerchief headbands. All are wrapped in their blankets. All are ready for work.

The War Captain is in charge. The men dig and hoe and shovel in a rhythm of movement and color timed to their singing.

In the pueblo, all is aflutter. The women, too, are dressed for the occasion in snowy, deerskin leggings and moccasins, short, full skirted dresses, bright-colored blouses, and calico shawls. The food is ready— stews of meat and chili, beans, golden-colored fried bread, blue-corn tortillas.

At midday they form a long line, sedate, serious, with only a hint of laughter. With bundles of food on their heads and cooking pots of stew in their hands, they walk single file across the earth-humped fields and

71

through the dry arroyos. At the end of the line is the teacher, lugging a huge pot of coffee, and the school-children follow, each grade bringing its offerings—canned milk and a parcel of sugar, apples and raisins, ginger cookies, all government issue.

At last they meet the men, who come singing and swinging along, still cleaning the ditches. The women place the food on blankets on the ground. The men stop working, and after long prayers are said, they eat the food the women have prepared for them. The women sit to one side, patiently waiting their turn. When the

men have finished, they sit in the shade of the stunted
piñons, smoke, and tease the women and children,
who finish what food there is left.

The men go on to clean the feeder ditches. The
women go back to the village to prepare tomorrow's
food. The teacher and the schoolchildren trudge off to
lessons and to books.

Ditch-cleaning takes two days, sometimes three. After this, there is a quiet time until the day when the
Summer Chief and the Winter Chief bless the mother
ditch with prayer and song, with offerings of corn pol-

len, turkey feathers, and a sprinkling of black earth—
marking the ceremonial road down the ditch center
where the water will run deepest, marking the ceremonial road straight and true; asking Avanyu, the Sacred Water Serpent, to come fast, bringing a swift flow
of water. The gate from the mountain to mother ditch
is opened, and water flows through it. The prayers of
the Winter Storm People have been answered. The
snows of long-winter fell often and heavy in the mountain highlands, filling the deep-walled canyons. The
prayers of the Summer Chief and the Winter Chief have
been answered. Sun Father has turned in his path, melting the snow in the canyons to cascading torrents, flooding the mountain lakes and the streams. The stars in
the sky have appeared at their proper times, fortelling
a year with water.

February has ended. March has come.

❀ ❀ ❀ ❀ ❀

The Unshared Days

March brings blustering winds like those of February,
but the days and nights are warmer. Snow melts on the
hillsides, uncovering red earth, bright and clean. The

willows' slender branches show a first faint greening, and the cottonwood trees begin to leaf. Mountain canyons overflowing with melted snow water festoon every cliffside and rock ridge with ribbons of waterfalls. The Winter Chief has given the pueblo into the hands of the Summer Chief, making it his right and his work, his privilege and his responsibility, to keep the days for the Tewa people.

On the day of this seasonal transfer, all the women of the Winter People and all the women of the Summer People bring their seed baskets to the house of the Summer Chief. Their baskets are filled with the seeds of the garden plants and the field crops that they selected in the harvest of autumn and kept safe in the months of the winter. They bring their baskets with reverence, with humility, but also with joy that they, being Indian women, are the keepers of the seeds, as they are the holders of life for their people.

The Summer Chief blesses each basket with prayer and sprinkles it with holy medicine, taking a handful of the seeds it holds to stuff the deerskin ball for ceremonial shinny.

Unshared days pass by, not lightly passed or in idleness, but in work and prayer, in ritual and retreat. This is a solemn time, a hushed, a holy time, the most sacred portion of the Tewa year, when the sun and the moon and the stars, water and wind are invoked by man to help Earth Mother receive the seeds of the corn plant, the squash, and the beans. Days pass by unshared with those who do not know and cannot understand the unity of life—the oneness of plants and animals and man.

Wind lulls in rest. Daylight begins earlier, lasts longer. Sunset colors linger to welcome the first stars of evening.

From a housetop the crier calls the news of the day. He calls the news to the people: "Make ready. Prepare yourselves. Prepare the things you will need. In four days the ball will be dropped." Again and again he repeats his call: "In four days the ball will be dropped." From the mountains comes the echo: four days . . . four days . . . four days.

The women begin to cook.

THE
DAYS
OF
THE
SUMMER

* * * * *

Time of Ceremonial Shinny

The first game of shinny opens the spring planting ceremonials. Both men and women play the game, most of
the time separately but occasionally together. They
each have their own deerskin ball: the one the men use
is filled with seeds; the women's ball is stuffed with deer
hair. The non-Indian neighbor may watch, if he chances
to come to the pueblo while the game is being played,
but almost never is he asked to play. Ceremonial shinny
belongs to the people. They know its significance. They
have inherited it from the Ancients.

On the morning of the fourth day after the crier has
announced to the people that "the ball will be

dropped," the Tewa, dressed in their best attire, stand in the plaza—waiting. The hushed merriment, the controlled gaiety of the crowd can be felt as vividly as the people can be seen. They are happy, alert, expectant, but neither restless nor noisy. They are waiting.

Today there is no wind. Except on the distant mountain peaks, the winter snow has melted. Doors are open. Sunlight fills the plaza. The air is blue, bright, sparkling, alive almost, with a buoyancy that lifts up heart and body of the men creatures of earth.

The Summer Chief, stern, proud, dressed in ceremonial leggings and blanket, stands on the roof of his house. The people in the plaza look up at him, their respected, beloved Old Father who now keeps the days for their good. He lifts high his arms, with both hands holding the seedball for all to see. The people wait, their eyes turned upward to the Summer Chief. He drops the ball, and at once the plaza is filled with leaping men and boys trying to catch it. At once the plaza is filled with running women and children as they rush into their houses, leaving the doors wide open. A man catches the ball, runs with it into his house, where his woman sprinkles it with corn meal before it is taken outside to be thrown again. The children of the household toss gifts into the plaza: meat, bread, apples, perhaps a box of store-bought cookies. Again and again the ball is thrown, batted, and caught, until it has been carried into every house and blessed with corn meal by every house-mother.

Then the seedball is taken into the fields, the men running west, north, east, and south, batting it from person to person until at last some man is lucky enough to burst it, scattering its precious seeds. The man so favored by good omen, having burst the ball, gives in thanksgiving a feast to all the people in the village.

After the seedball has been burst, the women begin their shinny game with a deerskin ball stuffed with deer hair. They do not go into the fields but run, also counter-sunwise, around their houses. They are as much in earnest as the men were and have as much fun batting and catching. They are also as skillful. Even with babies wrapped in the shawls upon their backs, they run as swiftly, leap as gracefully, and their game is as rough and as laughter-filled as any of the seedball players'. Their game, too, lasts until the ball bursts, scattering the deer hair. The woman whose clip bursts the ball will be awarded a gift of wild meat from the Kachinas, messengers from the spirit world, when they come to the pueblo.

In the springtime of the year, everyone who still can see and still can run plays ceremonial shinny—men and women, boys and girls, Old Fathers, Old Mothers, everyone plays. The very young children have their own shinny games. Their small shinny sticks are blessed with the same traditional prayer and the same ancient ritual as the shinny sticks of their elders. Babies not yet walking view the game from the folds of their mothers' blankets.

In a week or so, the shinny games are over. Their part in the slow unfolding of the year has been completed. Everything is right in the Tewa world. The "sun has been pulled to the south." Avanyu has "come fast" with the melted snow waters from the mountains' deep canyons. The seeds from the seedball have been scattered. The deer hair from the women's shinny ball has been blown in little tufts and wisps around the houses and across the plaza. The Tewa are ready for the next step along their year-trail.

The most sacred and most secret time of the Tewa, the time of ritual and ceremony for the germination and growth of all living things, has come. This is a time of deep devotion and special tenderness, when the Indian turns his thoughts and his acts to Earth Mother and away from the alien world that surrounds him. This is a time of special invocation to the sun and the moon and the stars, to the wind and the rain, for their aid in the continuation of life. This is a time when the Tewa shows his deep feeling for Earth Mother, who has held his Ancients, who has held him and, he hopes, the children who will follow him, close to her heart. In the Days-of-the-Old (and perhaps still) it was the custom for the horses to go unshod and for the people to wear soft-soled moccasins and use wooden tools rather than heavy equipment in planting, so that Earth Mother during her time of receiving the seeds of plant life might not be trampled upon or bruised.

A non-Indian world surrounds the Indian, engulfs him, changes him. It may be well that from time to time he still has the power to turn his thoughts and his actions inward, creating for himself a dormant period when the stresses and strains, the frustrations and anxieties of a way of life he did not choose cannot bruise or trample his spirit.

March withdraws and April enters.

✿ ✿ ✿ ✿ ✿

The Six-Day Ceremony

The red plum thicket puts out new leaves. The giant cottonwoods deck themselves in lacy green. The apricot trees begin to flower. The Indians worry. "Too warm," they say, "too warm."

The Winter Chief strengthens his prayers. The Summer Chief reviews the records of the days that have been counted. The shadows of morning and evening have fallen where they have been supposed to fall. The stars have come out in their right order. The first rays of sunrise and the last rays of sunset are as the Ancients predicted they would be. The omens for the planting season are good. The Summer Chief strengthens his prayers and continues his counting of the days.

The people keep to themselves. They do not go into town. They do not visit their neighbors on the other side of the river. If visitors come to the village, every Indian disappears into his house. The pueblo looks as if no one lives there or has ever lived there.

At school the children are preoccupied with other things rather than books. The teacher tells them in English, "You have spring fever." The children say in Tewa, "Even she knows that the spring time of the year has come upon us."

On a certain sundown the crier appears on the rooftop of his house and Indians fill the plaza to hear him tell them that in four days begins the Six-Day Ceremony that precedes the time of planting. The call is a lengthy one. Every man, woman, and child listens to what the crier tells them, although they have heard it many times before. The singsong voice is the same as it has always been, rising and falling in a hypnotic rhythm of high-pitched syllables, shrill yet musical. The words are the same. They have never been changed, nor must they ever be. The instructions are the same, given in the same sequence. Yet the people listen as they have listened for as long as they can remember and as their Ancients have listened in the shadowed ages of the past.

The women begin to cook, but on this occasion they do not work together as a village group. They divide

themselves into three groups to prepare three different foods, relatives working with relatives. The kinds of food are traditional, and they are prepared according to the ways that were used in the Days-of-the-Old.

This Six-Day Ceremony is mysterious, secret—a part of the design of the culture pattern seen only by the initiates. Not all the people see all the ceremonies. The Winter People see the part that belongs only to them; the Summer People see their portion. The non-Indian knows nothing of the ceremony. Even its name, "Shoots Magic," mystifies him. He hears nothing and he sees only the final dance, which is performed publicly in the plaza.

The first three days of the Shoots Magic Ceremony are the wood-gathering days. On the first day, wood is gathered for the Summer Chief. At sunrise the men and boys leave the plaza, the Old Fathers in ceremonial dress, the younger men in blue-jeans, bright-colored shirts and store-bought shoes. All but the schoolboys wear the traditional kerchief headband. They go in prescribed formation and in predetermined direction. At nightfall they return to the plaza carrying wood bundles on their backs in the way it has always been done for ceremonial wood-gathering. They go to the house of the Summer Chief, leaving for his use the wood they have brought down from the mountain slopes, and eat the food that has been prepared for them—corn without salt.

On the second day, in like manner but in a different direction, the men go forth to gather wood for the Winter Chief. Returning at nightfall, they leave the wood bundles at the door of his house and eat a mush made of young plant sprouts.

On the third day, the men go again in a third direction. The wood gathered on this day is for the Governor; the food eaten is chili and meat.

On the fourth day, from sunrise until sunset, no Indian is seen or heard. The excuse given to inquisitive neighbors is that "they are somewhere doing work." With the first star of evening, lamplight glows in the windows of the houses of the Summer People, but the Winter Peoples' houses are without light of any kind. With the gathering darkness, shadowy figures pass by the lamplighted windows, on their way to the kiva of the Winter People. The drum begins to pound and keeps on pounding through the hours of the night, until dawn brings the fifth-day ceremony.

On the fourth night, the Winter Kachinas come to the kiva of the Winter People and dance for them. The Summer People are not present.

Kachinas are supernatural beings who were created during that time when The People emerged from the underground world where they had been living to this, their present world. Kachinas are the messengers from earth people to the All-Powerful-Ones on whom earth people are dependent. Many of the Indians' legends of creation say that some of the emerging people fell into the waters held by the new world and became Kachinas, and for this reason they are the bringers of rain.

The fifth day is similar to the fourth, except that the Summer People are honored by the Summer Kachinas dancing for them.

On the sixth day, the pueblo is quiet. The people "are somewhere doing their work." At school, both the Summer People children and the Winter People children nod sleepily over their lessons. The English words that were easy to read last week are completely unrecognizable today. The small problems that were fun to solve elude them today. Their eyes are heavy. Their minds drowse. At last, one by one, they lay their tired heads on their flat-topped desks and give themselves to sleep. The teacher looks at the unfinished lessons and at the sleeping children. She looks at the mountains outside the schoolroom window, the enduring mountains unchangeable yet seemingly changing in contour, color, closeness with the changing light of the sun and the shadows of the clouds. Suddenly the book in her hand is heavy, weighted with values that are as necessary as the rain for today's existence and are as difficult for the Indian children to understand as it is for her to understand the dancing for rain.

After nightfall a long line of dark-blanketed men leaves the pueblo, walking into the night. By the first light of dawn they will reach a special place near a certain mountain peak where the blue spruce grows tall and heavily branched. They spend the day selecting the branches they will need, separating them from the mother trees. At sunset they have all they need and begin the long walk home to their mud-walled town in the sandhills.

At dawn the next morning they enter the plaza and the kiva like a moving forest of spruce. On their spruce-gathering journey they have had neither food nor water, nor have they killed the game that watched them so curiously while they worked.

By mid-morning they are ready for the climax of the Shoots Magic Ceremony. They are ready to dance in the plaza. The dance may be seen and its joy shared by Indian and non-Indian alike.

✿ ✿ ✿ ✿ ✿

Time of Mystery

April continues as it began, with bright, warm, still days. The trees and the thickets, the wild rosebushes and the rabbit brush have come into leaf. The Indians say, "Too warm for now." The Winter Chief strengthens his prayers. The Summer Chief watches the stars of the night and the shadows of the day.

Nothing must mar this mystic time of year. The earth must be ready to receive the seeds of the plants. The days and the nights must be neither too warm nor too cold. The wind must not be too violent, drying the moisture from the land. There must be harmony among the sun, moon, stars and the earth so that the seeds may germinate and the plants grow. The Summer Chief watches and counts and is unperturbed. The omens are good. The stars have said that rain will come and crops will grow.

Members of the Medicine Society go at night to the fields to "sweep" them clean of those things that could bring harm. They can do this because they have the power to expel the forces of evil that can cause not only individual illness but common misfortune.

The Society of Fun Makers, associates of the Kachina rain-bringers, have at this time special rites. The men of the Hunt Society fast and pray. The War Society members, who are in spiritual charge of the food supply, invoke the All-Powerful Ones to bring the plants to fruitful harvest. Immediately after ceremonial shinny, the Women's Society gives its dance. There are special rituals for the planting of corn and the planting of wheat, and of beans.

April brings the Christian Holy Week, commemorating the passion and crucifixion of Christ. At this time in some pueblos roads are blocked and a guard is stationed on a house roof. The non-Indian visitor is not permitted to come into the village. He does not know if his way is barred because a prayer is being enacted for the grief of the Christian world at the crucifixion of Christ or whether there is a continuation of the invocation of planting.

From summer solstice until the seeds are resting in the earth of the fields, the Indian is much too busy to be bothered with his non-Indian neighbors. He neither explains nor denies his concern for Earth Mother from whose heart his people ascended at the time of their emergence into this present world, Earth Mother who sustains them in life and who receives them in death. How could non-Indians understand, the Old Fathers reason—they who cut the earth with the steel blades of a plow and cast the seeds of planting by machine?

But the young Indian men know that they straddle two worlds. They know that they can adjust to their environment. Indians have always been able to adjust to their environment. They know, too, that adjustment is a slow process and that the Old Ones of every world and every time fight change.

So the days of March have become part of the past, and most of the days of April. Holy Thursday comes, and Good Friday, and many pueblo roads are still barred from outside intrusion. But on Easter Sunday the roads are open. The Indians crowd their small churches to celebrate joyfully the day of the risen Christ. On Easter afternoon there is a dance ceremonial in the plaza. Oftentimes the Buffalo Dance or the Deer Dance is given. Neighbors, friends, and tourists come to watch a ceremony as old in meaning and in pattern as time, and as new in precision and perfection as the theater of tomorrow.

* * * * *

Time of Planting

In the high foothill country of the Rockies, May often comes in with a blizzard. Snow drifts against house walls, rests in thick fluffy patches on the leafy branches of the trees and the tips of the bushes, wraps the roads and the fields under a white coverlet. It lasts only a day and a night. By next day's noon the snow has melted completely. The air is clean-smelling, the earth spongy with stored moisture, the buds swollen with water. The omens for a good growing year are still holding.

May races begin. Young men, strong and swift, their lithe, brown bodies glistening with the mists of morning, streak through the gray dawn like the first rays of sunlight. Straight, slender, laughing young girls watch their young men's departure and run swiftly to meet them as they return.

In a Keres village the young men racers run along the river bank kicking a stick before them as they run to mark high on the sandy bank a line the water must reach to quench the summer thirst of their crops.

In a Tewa village they run along a race course that has been trodden deep by the running feet of their fathers and their grandfathers' fathers.

In a Tigua village the young men race on the slopes of the mountains that rise abruptly on the edges of the village.

After the races are over, the fields are blessed. As in many Pueblo customs borrowed from the early Spanish, the blessing of the fields is partly Christian, wholly Indian. The statue of San Ysidro, patron saint of the *milpa,* is carried in procession through the fields. Corn pollen is sprinkled before his trail, and paper flowers fill the pathway behind him. With San Ysidro is his plow and his angel companion, carved in wood. Every child has heard the Old Fathers tell the story of San Ysidro, his angel, and his plow. "San Ysidro asked God for an angel to do his plowing while he, San Ysidro, prayed." The children laugh. They know what is coming, but they never tire of hearing it again and again. "And God told San Ysidro, 'I'll send you an angel to pray and you do your plowing.'" The children love San Ysidro. He seems close to them.

After the fields are blessed and the earth has been prepared to receive the seeds, planting takes place. The fields are held in common by the men of the pueblo. Together they plant them with corn, chili, squash, and beans.

Immediately after planting, there are rain pilgrimages to sacred lakes and to shrines at sacred springs that are hidden away in the canyons surrounded by bare rock peaks of the Sangre de Cristo Mountains. Not everyone may make a pilgrimage for rain; only those who have received the right by vow or dedication or membership in a certain society and who have received training in the special rituals and prayers necessary for the bringing of rain.

Now that the fields have been planted, the men must cultivate and irrigate, from sunrise to sunset, day after day. Each tender new plant is sheltered from a too harsh sun ray or a too strong wind by little mounds of earth or of brush. Feeder ditches are dug from the mother ditch along each corn row, and water is run through them. Then little earth dams are made, to block the flow and divert the water to another row. The water in the feeder ditches must run in a steady trickle, strong enough to water each thirsty plant, but not so strong that tender roots are harmed. Each trickle of water must be watched by a man with a hoe who must be poised ready to hurry it onward by digging deeper or to stop its flow by a small earth clod. At this time of the growing-year, irrigation never stops. The plants are always thirsty and the dry land is greedy for water.

Sun Father rises earlier, sets later. The days are warm, but the nights are cool. The mountain peaks are still snow-rimmed. Mountain crevices are snow-packed. Icicles hang from the cliff ledges in long, heavy fringes of iridescent glass. The canyon walls are streaming in ribbons of waterfalls. On the floors of the canyon, snow melts and rushes along in the cracks of the rocks, filling the mountain lakes to overflow and flooding the narrow mountain streams. The water in the mother ditch runs swift and strong. The little feeder ditches trickle their water to the rows of corn and the bean plants and the squash and the chili.

The Pueblo women coil pottery, decorate and fire it, walk to the town market to sell it and buy lard and salt, sugar and coffee. Daily they take food and water to the hungry men working the milpas. The boys work beside their fathers in the fields. The girls, carrying younger children on their backs, help their mothers in the never ending work of every day.

The days are sunny, warm, and dry. "Too dry," the Indians say, looking at the cloudless sky. "There should be rain by now," they say. "There should be rain." Again certain Indians make the rain pilgrimage to the sacred lake and the shrine at the sacred spring.

The days grow longer, warmer. In the mountains, only the peaks are rimmed with snow; the icicles and the snow packs have melted. Nothing is left of the waterfalls but wet streaks on the canyon walls. The lakes are smaller. The mountain streams have run their course. The dry, sandy soil of the mountain slopes has soaked up the flood water. The water in mother ditch is lower, slower. It takes longer for the trickle of water in the feeder ditches to reach the end of a corn row.

June comes and with it the pounding of the drums.

Beginning of Long-Summer

In the country of the northern Rio Grande, June is one of the two perfect months of the year. June days are bright and warm—but, even in midday, not too warm —with an underlying coolness, a last reminder of the melting snow on the mountain peaks. Skies are blue and cloudless. There is no wind, not even a breeze, to ruffle the tranquillity of the sun-filled days. Every sand hump and arroyo bank is carpeted with wild flowers, great patches of blue verbena and scarlet Indian paintbrush and miniature yellow flowers and white and pink ones, small and perfect but without fragrance, as if all their strength had been spent in coming into blossom in the dry, sandy soil.

Wild gourd vines creep along the ground in a tangle of stems and leaves. At the first appearance of a gourd, the Indian begins to shape it to his need. Gently he shapes the young gourd to the form he wants it to have at its harvest, to be used as a rattle, bowl, or dipper, or for headdress flowers or knobs or horns.

In the fields, the young corn plant is thrusting up new tender shoots and the beans and the chili have begun their growing. There is still enough water in mother ditch to send forth little trickles in the feeder ditches up and down the rows of corn. In this quiet interim period between the flood waters of melted snow and the rains of long-summer, if they come, there can be time for play —a short time, only a day, but a day filled with delight. The Pueblo Indian loves to play. Along with his love of laughter, his keen sense of humor, and his power of mimicry, he likes to use his physical skills. For his play day, while the corn is growing, the Indian goes to the Pueblo of San Juan. Tigua, Tewa, Keres, and Jemez all go to San Juan to help the Indians of that village celebrate Saint John's Day, the feast of their patron saint.

There is the usual church service, the procession carrying the saint to his plaza bower, and later in the day an Indian dance ceremonial, perhaps the Eagle Dance or the Deer Dance. But the attraction of midday is playing a game taught them by the early Spanish, a game they have kept through the centuries as their special name-day celebration.

The English name for the game is "rooster pull." It is played by two teams of young men riding bareback on their frisky cow ponies. The Spanish taught them to play the game with a live rooster tied securely in a small bag, only its neck and head protruding. At a signal, all the riders ride as fast as their horses can run to a pile of sand where the rooster has been partially buried. The lucky man reaches down from his horse and "pulls" the rooster from the sand without changing his horse's

97

speed. The game is for members of one team to snatch or "pull" the rooster from members of the rival teams, until one man holds the "last feather." His team is declared winner.

The game is daring, fast, rough, and cruel for horses, riders, and rooster. However, in late years a bag half full of sand, rooster-size and of rooster weight, is substituted for the live bird. The non-Indian visitors seem to like the sandbag better, but for the Indian participant the live rooster proved more difficult and therefore more enjoyable to cope with than the bag half filled with sand.

After the game is finished, everyone watches the dance ceremonial as the hot afternoon sun beats down on the sun-baked plaza. At sunset the visiting Indians return to their home villages and by sunrise they are once more out in their fields cultivating, irrigating, and watching, watching for the rains to come and the corn to grow.

The warm, still days of June slip by under a blazing sun in a cloudless sky.

Before the end of the month, the drums begin to beat in the kivas of the pueblos of the northern country of the Rio Grande. In all the plazas of the flat-roofed, mud-walled towns, sometime during these last days of long-summer's beginning, the people will give a dance that has "belonged" to them since time began.

The Tigua people of Isleta and Picuris and Taos give

the Dance of the Evergreen. Although similar dances having other names are given by other groups, theirs is Evergreen Dance. It "belongs" to them.

For this dance, the branches of the Douglas fir are used, the Douglas fir that grows only in the high slopes of the Rockies, close to the timber line. The branches must be cut at a certain time of day in a certain way and carried back into the pueblo after the next day's dawning. The costuming of the dancers, the dance steps, and the dance formation are similar for all the groups that give the ceremonial. But those who gather the branches differ among the different villages. In some pueblos, only the ceremonial Fathers make the mountain journey to cut the spruce. Often when the distance is only twenty or thirty miles all the dancers go, but in distant pueblos, where the trek to the mountain high places is greater, runners must be sent.

The prayer for this dance, intoned at the cutting, is a petition to the spirit-mother of the tree to spread her branches—her arms wide—covering the world with rain. There is also another invocation to the All-Powerful Ones who live in the world beneath this present one, close to the heart of Earth Mother, to expel their holy breath upward, through the soil of the earth, upward through the tree roots, the trunk, branches, and leaves, to become billowing, banking rain clouds heavy with rain.

About noon, when the sun stands on his own shadow,

the dancers appear at the edge of the plaza. There may be as few as twenty and as many as fifty boys and men. Small boys, no older than nine or ten, are at both ends of the line, which graduates toward the middle in size and age from boy to youth to man and, at the exact center, to the Ceremonial Father, the dance leader.

The dancers are led by the Fun Makers and attended by the War Captain and his assistants. For a heartbeat of time, the dancers stand motionless like a forest of young fir trees covering a mountain slope. Over the white Hopi kilt, tied with the white woven rain sash, each dancer wears a skirt of swishing evergreen branches. A wreath of evergreen is around his neck, and sprays of the dark green needles are tied to his arms. Beneath his knees are yarn-tied turtle-shell rattles. Around the skirt of spruce is a belt of bells.

The leader is wrapped in a blanket, with a wreath of cornhusks on his head, symbol of cloud mist. He begins to stamp, shaking his dried gourd rattle, and the pebbles inside it sound, as they should, like the patter of rain.

With the leader's stamp, the long line shifts, spacing itself. Almost imperceptibly, like a mountain breeze running lightly through the branches of the fir trees, the line begins to sway. From each side of center to the smallest boys at either end, in perfect unison, the long line sways. The stamping and the swaying quickens. The line begins to dance to their own singing and the pounding of the drum. The belted bells and the shells of the turtles make an accompaniment of sound to the patter of raindrops in the dried gourd rattles.

Sun Father moves slowly across the sky until the moment of sunset, when the dance is finished. The dancers take their skirts and wreaths and sprays of spruce to Mother Earth to feed its water, but the mother ditch is almost dry. They go to the river to cast their gift upon its surface, but its narrow stream is too weak to carry the weight of the branches.

The spruce that was cut with invocation, that was carried according to the pattern from the mountain slopes to the pueblo kiva, that was worn in the dance ceremonial, cannot be lightly thrown aside. The children of the earth had petitioned the spirit-mother of the evergreen to open wide her arms to cover the world with rain. These branches now must be returned to the spirit-mother to act as messengers to the Giver-of-Rain.

At last the dancers find a spot in a deep arroyo to bury the skirts and the wreaths and the sprays of the fir tree. As they cover the branches with the damp sand, they petition Avanyu, the Sacred Water Serpent, to come fast with the rain.

Sunset colors fade. The sky grows gray and somber. Toward the distant mountains, rain clouds gather. The people are satisfied. All is well. The Giver of Water has heard their prayers. Clouds must come before the rain.

June edges into July. Long-summer envelops the land.

✿ ✿ ✿ ✿ ✿

Ceremonials of Long-Summer

The mystic and symbolic ritual of Indian prayer ceremonials is always complex and often difficult for the
non-Indian to understand, but the religious beliefs
which govern them are basic and more easily grasped.
The Indian believes that nature is a manifestation of
the supernatural and that drama is a manifestation of
prayer. He believes in the unity of life as manifested in
all things. He believes in a twofold principle of existence as manifested in the working together of male and
female.

His year is divided into two parts, winter and summer. His ceremonials are divided into two parts, ceremonials of winter and the spring-summer rituals. God
and nature are one. Drama and prayer are one.

The winter dances are portrayals of the first belief:
the unity of life. By pantomime and drama, by impersonation and mimicry, by petition and invocation, the
Indian asks his animal brothers to sacrifice themselves
so that man, their brother, may have continuing life.
The impersonators are men who take on the image of
the animals; the only women in the ceremonial are the
spirit-mothers of the animals in whose honor the dance
is given.

The dancers are the actors; the onlookers are the audience; each group keeps to its own role. When the dancer puts on the animal image, he becomes that animal. The onlooker views the dance as if it were a theater production; he revels in the mysticism, delights in the color and design and rhythm.

The spring and summer dances are invocations to the All-Powerful Ones to make the seed take hold and the crops come to fruition. As many women as men dance in recognition of the dual principles of all existence. The men dance vigorously, stamping the ground; the women shuffle, patting the dust with bare, brown feet. The men dance to the women, around them, and from them. The women, holders of life, keep time to their stamping, with evergreen sprays, symbol of life, held in their hands.

These summer dances neither impersonate nor dramatize. The dancers dance a prayer—a primitive, hypnotic, visible prayer. Sound and rhythm, movement and color all blend together. Everything about the dance and the dancers is symbolic: the evergreen, the gourds, the corn, and feathers, the shells and bells, and the colors of the yarns used to tie them. All present participate in the strength of the prayer and the benefits it grants—dancers and watchers, Sun Father and Earth Mother, clouds and rain, seed and life, germination and fruition. All are involved.

* * * * *

Dancing for Rain

The heat of the sun engulfs the land, burning everything it touches: the hard, cracked earth, the sand-
filled roads, the crumbling bank of the dry wash. The
sky is empty of clouds. Heat haze like a blanket of
smoke hangs heavy over the foothills.

The People Who Bring the Storms have gone again
on a pilgrimage for rain. The Winter Chief keeps to
his house, alone with his prayers. The Summer Chief
watches the sunrise and the shadows, the sunsets and
the stars. The kiva drums are calling. Far into the night
the sound of their beats makes a background for the
pebble-patter of the gourds. The Tewa people of Santa
Clara give the Rainbow Dance, which has always "belonged" to them.

Two men, two women dance to the drum and the
singing of the chorus. The chorus outnumbers the
dancers two to one. On their backs the women dancers
wear a kind of shield of many colors bordered with the
tips of eagle feathers. In their hands they hold the symbol of life, the sprays of evergreen. The men's bodies
are painted black, with a band of white across their
shoulders. Like the women's shields, their faces are

painted in many colors and a fan of eagle feathers is tied in their shining, long, black hair.

The men dancers carry the rainbows, arches of willow wands painted in rainbow colors and tied with eagle down. In unison the men stamp the earth; in unison they raise the willow wands and jump through their arches, stamping the earth as they touch the ground.

July slips into August. The land is dry, Mother Ditch is dry, the river is dry. The wild flowers fold in their petals and the corn droops in the fields. The air is still and dry; not a breath of wind, not a drop of moisture soothes the burned earth or the corn or the people.

The Bringers-of-the-Storm return from their pilgrimage. The Hunt Society goes to a shrine at a hidden spring that no one but their members knows about. They clean the ritual road to the spring so that nothing may hamper the water spirit when it comes, bringing the gift of water.

In the kivas the drums are pounding and in the plazas the bare feet of the dancers slap the earth the way the drummer slaps the drum. The people of the northern Rio Grande country are dancing for rain, are calling the rain, are petitioning the rain to come.

In a Keres village, two hundred dancers pour out of the kiva and come into the plaza in two long lines, one of men, one of women. A chorus of fifty chanters accompanies the dancers, marking time with their hands and the stamp of their feet. The leader carries a pole tied with streamers of many colors and topped with yellow feathers. The leader dips his pole and turns it and dips it again and sways it over the heads of the dancing people. The women move the sprays of evergreen up and down to the pounding of the drum, to the swaying of the pole and the slapping of bare feet on the sun-baked earth.

The drumbeats pound, the voices of the chanters pound, the slap of the stamping feet pounds. The spectators draw closer to the dancers, closer to the chanters, become one with the pounding of the drum and the feet. The earth vibrates with sound. The air pulses with sound. The sky covers itself with clouds and the clouds bend down, bend down, heavy with the rain they hold.

A flash of lightning, a bolt of thunder; the clouds break and the rain pours down. The drum keeps pounding, the feet keep stamping, and the rain pours down, pours down, wetting the dry earth, filling the river and the ditches, giving life to the corn, refreshing the people, who seem unaware of its falling.

The dance ends, but the rains continue. The wild flowers unfold their petals, the mountain grass grows thick, the canyons are robed in green, and the mountain slopes are drenched. The corn grows tall, matures, ripens.

The Winter Chief comes from his house. The Summer Chief rests his eyes from watching the signs of the shadows and stars. The good omens have held. The year has been heavy with water and the corn is ready to harvest.

* * * * *

Time of the Harvest

The months of autumn come to the mountain country, into its foothills, across its plains, and into the pueblos of the northern Rio Grande. The days are golden, warm, and still, and the nights glow softly under the silver light of the harvest moon. The high mountain slopes of somber green spruce and pine show patchwork of dazzling yellow where the thick groves of tall, slender aspen trees, nursemaids to the baby evergreen, stretch their golden-leafed branches heavenward. In the mountain meadows, wild turkeys feast on the ripe, red berries of the kinnikinnick hiding under the ground-oak cover of scarlet, bronze, and copper-colored leaves. Doe and fawn romp and frolic in the tall grass as elk standing knee-deep in the fern beds watch their play. A bear and her cub try to strip a blueberry bush, eating greedily its lush sweet berries. On a rock ledge a mountain goat leans far over the knife-sharp edge of its narrow perch to peer down curiously at a herd of antelope outrunning the wind on the plain below.

In the foothills the stunted piñon trees are heavy with cone-filled nuts, and bright-blue berries cling to the gray lacy branches of the cedars. Bluejays scold and chatter. Jack rabbits and cottontails play hide-and-seek among the purple asters. Ground squirrels fight with the woodpeckers over every rose tip and seed pod. Along the sandy banks of the river, the chamisa bushes are top-heavy under their golden crowns. The willows and the plum thicket still retain their summer elegance, but high above them the green leaves of the cottonwood trees are streaked and splotched with yellow.

Between the river and the fields are the round threshing pens piled high with the dried bean plants. Small boys run their horses around and around in the pens to thresh the beans by trodding them. The air is filled with the choking dust of the dry plant stems and leaves, the smell of horse sweat and boy sweat, and the joyful yells of the enthusiastic threshers.

Young women also are here at the threshing pens, where they winnow the beans brought to them by the boys. Holding the winnowing baskets high above their heads, they pour pounded leaves and stems and beans onto the squares of canvas on the ground at their feet. The little wind of autumn carries the dried stalks away.

In the pueblo, only the blue doors of the houses can be seen. The house walls are completely hidden by

108

strings of scarlet chili peppers hanging from the extending roof vigas to touch the ground. Spread out to dry in the autumn sunshine on the flat roofs are piles of pumpkins, oddly shaped gourds, rows of squash cut into quarter moons, and halves of apricots.

The pueblo plaza full of laughter and color seems like a carnival of autumn. The men bring loads of ripe corn ears and pile them in hills before the doors of their women's houses. Blue, purple-blue, red, pink, yellow, white, and lavender, each ear is perfect with its even rows of colored corn kernels.

While the corn plants were growing in the milpa, they were men's property, men's work, and men's responsibility; but mature and fruitful, they become the property of women. Now that the corn has been piled before the doors of their houses, it becomes women's responsibility and women's work. The women are the ones who select the seed corn for next year's planting and the food corn for winter eating.

This is the gayest, happiest, busiest time of the year. The house-mothers sit behind their piles of corn in the bright sunshine in the plaza, teasing their men as each new load is brought. But while they tease, they also work. Folding back the husks from each cob with sure and gentle fingers, they sort each ear for size, for color, for perfection, and for use. Soon there are many little piles around the larger one. There is a small pile for the sacred corn meal and one for the seed corn. Much of the corn will be tied by its husks into bunches or ladders and hung from the vigas of the house storeroom for winter use. Some will be roasted in deep-dug pits lined with hot stones, and eaten at once for harvest feasting. Some will be soaked in lye water made of juniper ashes and eaten as hominy. Some will be parched in the out-of-doors ovens and some will be ground into corn meal on the stone metates. This work will be done by the young women. The older ones have had their years of grinding corn.

On the floor of the main room of every house, knee length from the outside walls, are three stone metates. Each metate is used for the grinding of one kind of corn-meal flour, coarse, medium or powder-fine. Kneeling on the floor by the metate, the soles of her feet braced flat against the house wall, and in her hands the smaller grinding stone, the young woman rubs the hard corn kernels into corn-meal flour. It is back-aching work, but Indian women take great pride in their skill at grinding. The young wife-to-be always grinds baskets of corn meal for her mother-in-law, to prove herself an industrious housewife.

In many of the villages it is a custom for the young men to sing to the grinders-of-corn while they work. The corn-grinding songs are as old as the art of corn-grinding. The words and the rhythm remain unchanged since the first singer sang them to his sweetheart to lighten her task of grinding the corn.

After the field crops are harvested and the apricots picked, the Old Mothers go into the sandhills and along the dry washes and the deep arroyos, gathering wild plants for food, for medicine, for dyes. The younger people go into the foothills to gather the piñon nuts from the stunted trees.

The highland country, foothills, sand dunes, and valley are bright with sunshine and laughter. The year has been a good one. The All-Powerful Ones have answered the chants and invocations. The Winter Chief and the Summer Chief have kept well the days for their people.

There is only one more autumn activity to be accomplished, one more thing to be done before the circle of seasons closes.

✽ ✽ ✽ ✽ ✽

The Circle Closes

The sounds of tom-tom, rattle, and gourds echo and re-echo from the distant mountains as Keres, Tigua, and Tewa people dance the Basket Dances of autumn. The women carry baskets decked with turkey or eagle feathers and filled with melons, corn, and bread, which they throw to the people watching the dance. The Fun Makers are out also, bringing laughter and throwing gifts of the fields to all who want them.

These Basket Dances are the people's way of returning in gratitude to Earth Mother some of the gifts she has been so lavish in giving them. They are the age-old portrayal of women as the holding vessels of life, just as the baskets they carry are the holding vessels of food for the living. They are prayers of thanksgiving and of joy in being able to return thanks to the Holders-of-the-Trails-of-Life.

It is appropriate that these last ceremonials of the year are given in joy for the living. At the conclusion of the last Basket Dance the drums stop pounding; the year is closed. The time has come for the transfer of the season and the counting of the days from the hands of the Summer Chief to the hands of the Winter Chief. Now he will be the one who watches the sun and the moon, the shadows and the stars. Now he will be the one who counts the days for his people's good.

Today is for the living. Tomorrow is the Day of the Dead. And the circle of seasons has closed around another year that has slipped into the past.